A **CAT'S EYE** Mystery

Mystery of Disaster Island

by ANN RIVKIN

SCHOLASTIC INC.
New York Toronto London Auckland Sydney Tokyo

ISBN 0-590-31803-9

12 11 10 9 8 7 6 5 4 3 2 1   12   3 4 5 6 7/8

Printed in the U.S.A.

Contents

The Ghostly Mansion

John woke early. At first, as he looked around, he didn't know where he was. What had happened to the pictures he had taped around his room? and the baseball mitt that hung above his bed? If Linda had been up to any of her tricks ...

Quickly he sat up in bed. But before his feet touched the floor, he remembered.

This was not his room. He was not in the house where he had lived all his life. He was in some strange place on the west coast of Canada — and even before he saw the place, before he found out anything about it, he knew he didn't want to live here.

He wanted to be back home with his friends and his Little League team and the life he had always known. But last spring the doctor had told his father: "No more cold Manitoba winters for you, Mr. Stafford. An open air life in a milder climate is what you need now."

The very next day Mrs. Stafford had called the three children together. "I've got something exciting to tell you," she had said. "Dad and I have decided that as soon as school is out we're going to move to the West Coast to live. To British Columbia. You'll see all kinds of things you've never seen before — mountains and ocean and dense forests with huge trees."

She had smiled brightly and tried to make it sound like an adventure, but John had hated the idea from the start. He hadn't wanted to say good-bye to his friends and leave the only home he had ever known. He hadn't even liked the jet they had flown to British Columbia. And he certainly didn't like this motel where they were staying until they found a place to live.

He was so full of discontent that he couldn't lie still. He dressed hurriedly in jeans and sweatshirt and tiptoed across the room, being careful not to wake anyone. Just outside the door he stopped dead in his tracks and stared.

When they had arrived at the motel last night, it had been dark, and they hadn't been able to see anything. Now John gazed at the blue waters spread out before him, dotted with

2

tree-covered islands of every size and shape. Off in the distance snow-capped mountains shone in the morning sun.

"Not bad, eh?" called a cheerful voice.

John spun around in surprise. He thought the rest of the family was still asleep, but there was his sister, Linda, sitting on an old tree stump near the water's edge, bursting with importance at being the first to discover this amazing spectacle.

John turned his head away. "I'd rather look at the muddy Red River," he grumbled.

"John Stafford, you ought to be ashamed," Linda scolded. "You were the one who told Rick and me that even if we didn't like it here we had to pretend for Dad's sake — and now look at you."

John's face turned red. "Dad isn't here to see me," he muttered. "I put on an act when he's around."

"Well, you'd better start acting now." Linda's voice became a whisper, and John looked up just in time to see his father coming toward them.

Mr. Stafford was tall and wiry, with brown hair. John resembled him, while Linda was small and blonde like their mother. Their little brother, Ricky, was somewhere in between.

"I see we don't need any alarm clock this

3

morning. It must be the sea breeze that does it." Mr. Stafford drew in a deep breath of the soft, salt air. "What would you like to do today?" he asked. "It's perfect weather to go out on the water."

John remembered about being cheerful for his father's sake, so he made his voice happy. "Can we rent a boat, do you think?"

His father looked pleased. "That's exactly what I was wondering," he said. "After breakfast we'll see about going out for the day to explore the coast. We'll cruise along, stopping wherever we like and exploring whatever looks interesting."

"It *all* looks interesting to me," their mother's voice broke in. She was coming toward them, holding onto Ricky who had been climbing around on the slippery rocks. "Maybe we'll see a place where we'd like to live," she said. "Anyone got any ideas? Where would you like to live, Rick?"

"In a lighthouse," Ricky shouted. They had seen a lighthouse on the way to the motel yesterday.

"In a houseboat," Linda said.

Mr. Stafford turned to John. "How about you, son?"

With his father's eyes on him, John had to think of something quickly. The only place he

4

really wanted to live was in the house they had just left, but he couldn't say that.

"On an island," he said. "A small one that would belong to us."

"Well," Mr. Stafford said, grinning at his three children, "maybe we can find a small island with a lighthouse on it and a houseboat at the dock. But it'll probably take a while, so we'd better not waste any time. Who's going to help get breakfast?"

Everyone lent a hand, and breakfast was soon on the table. Finally, after they did the dishes and tidied up the motel room, they were ready to leave.

They rented a boat with an outboard motor, and Mr. Stafford made sure that every member of the family put on a life jacket before they set out. He had served in the Navy, and was a stickler for water safety. He also knew all about tides and currents and studied a chart as he steered the boat.

Linda and her mother also had a map of the area, and they called out the names of the different islands as they passed. Ricky had taken command of his father's compass and kept announcing the direction at every small swerve of the boat.

Only John was silent. He had the binoculars and was supposed to report anything that

5

looked exciting. But he kept the glasses to his eyes without really looking through them. His mind was far away — with his friend Mike back home, and the empty lot behind his house where they used to practice pitching.

After a while Linda's voice brought John sharply back to the present. "Haven't you seen anything good yet?" she demanded. "Let me have the binoculars. I bet I could find a dozen interesting places in one minute."

For an instant John felt like throwing them at her. He almost said, "Here, take them. I don't care." If he had said it, all the things that happened afterward might never have happened at all.

But because of his father, John bit his tongue and turned his back on his sister. Pretending to be interested, he kept gazing through the binoculars, hating every bit of sea and rock he looked at. Then he suddenly gasped and sat up with a jerk.

"Wow!"

Instead of the summer homes and holiday resorts he had been scanning all morning, he now stared at an amazing sight — a ghostly log mansion seemed to be rising out of the mist!

John didn't have to pretend interest any more. In fact he leaned so far forward to get a better view that he nearly fell overboard. Grabbing him by his shirt and pulling him back, Linda cried, "What are you looking at? Let me see!"

Once again she reached for the glasses, but John pulled away. He wasn't going to part with them now that he had found something exciting. "You'll have to wait —"

He broke off abruptly. For as suddenly as it appeared, the vision had faded away. Desperately John tried to adjust the glasses — but it was no use. The strange log mansion was gone.

"Dad, turn the boat around and go slowly for a minute!"

"What do you see, son?" Pleased at John's interest, he quickly altered course.

John peered anxiously through the binoculars. He was sure he hadn't imagined the whole thing. It had been so clear. And it couldn't have been a mirage. You only saw mirages in the desert when you'd gone too long without water. So it must have been real!

"There it is! Stop!"

Mr. Stafford cut the motor, and when John handed him the glasses he whistled out loud. "Well — that is worth stopping for. I wonder what it is?"

By this time Linda was looking as though

she would burst wide open if she had to wait another minute. Mr. Stafford passed the glasses to her, and she gasped.

"Wow! A haunted castle!"

Then Ricky had to look too, though he didn't really know what he was seeing. At last Mrs. Stafford managed to have her turn.

For several minutes she gazed through the glasses. "I wonder . . ." she said thoughtfully. "Could it be one of the Long Houses that the Coast Indians used to build? If it is, it must be very old."

"I think it's a castle," Linda said. "I bet it's haunted and —"

"I don't know what it is," John broke in, "but I'd like to see it close up. Can we go and see it, Dad?"

"Well, we can try," replied his father, looking doubtfully through his maps and charts. "There's nothing about it in any of the guides, and I don't know if we'll be able to find it. But we'll sure try."

As the boat surged ahead, the log mansion disappeared again, but Mr. Stafford had noted the direction and he steered toward it. Eagerly John leaned forward. For the first time since he had said good-bye to his friends, he forgot about being homesick.

They were following a jagged coastline, and

each time they rounded a point the strange building reappeared, then vanished again. Whenever he spotted it, John yelled out and gave the new direction.

Ricky was absorbed watching a busy little tugboat towing logs, and Linda spent the time waving to people at the holiday resorts along the shore. But John never took his eyes away from the glasses.

Suddenly he gave a great shout. "There it is, around the bend!"

As Mr. Stafford nosed the boat into the narrow channel, they seemed to enter a different world. It was strangely quiet. No other boats, no laughing vacationers. Even the air seemed heavier. They all watched silently as the winding channel suddenly revealed a small island ahead.

John caught his breath. Although he couldn't see the mansion any more — he couldn't see anything except the trees that crowded down to the shore and a derelict wharf — he was sure this was the place. Unlike all the other islands they had passed, this one looked strange and unreal, like the vision he had seen through the glasses. Somehow he just *knew* the log building was there.

◆

A Deserted Island

As the boat nosed in toward the old wharf, John sat poised in the bow, ready to jump. Even before his father had tied up, he leapt ashore, startling a group of cormorants which flew out to sea with shrill cries. A squirrel scolded indignantly, and high in an alder tree a chickadee shouted at the intruders to go away.

"I guess they're not used to people around here." John found the idea exciting. Landing on a deserted island was a real adventure, even if civilization was only a short boat ride away.

Eagerly he made for the overgrown trail beneath the trees. Linda was close behind, with the others following. The path had once been broad and smooth, but now it was covered with thick brush, forming a green tunnel of growth. Nettles stung their hands as they broke their way through. Overhanging branches scratched at their cheeks and old roots made them stumble, but no one seemed to care.

"Can you see anything?" Linda panted. "Any sign of the haunted castle?"

John shook his head. He had no breath left for talking. Hurrying forward, he tripped over an old hemlock trunk lying across the path. As he got to his feet he saw that the tunnel ended in a clearing. And across the clearing, directly ahead, was the log mansion!

The building was even more amazing close up than it had been from a distance. A high balcony circled the top half of the structure, and above that was a steeply sloping roof made of bark. The massive front steps had been sliced from tree trunks and rose up to imposing double doors. In the bright sunshine the whole building glowed with a golden hue like something out of a fairy tale, inviting them in, yet at the same time warning them away.

A quivery feeling ran down John's spine. Linda clutched at his arm and he knew just how she felt. Even Ricky seemed to feel the strange atmosphere, for he stood quietly holding his mother's hand instead of jumping around as he usually did.

Surrounding the house was a large garden gone wild. Roses, honeysuckle, and columbine climbed all over each other, and flowers of every description grew upward and outward in a crazy quilt of color.

"This was never an Indian house," Mrs. Stafford said softly. "It's too big for a family home, but it might have been a hotel. I wonder—"

She stopped, but no one questioned her. Everyone was wondering the same thing. Who had built the mansion? What kind of people had lived here, and why had they abandoned it?

Leaving the others silently staring, John walked around the side of the house. There was a strange tantalizing scent in the air. Then he saw the tasty red shapes beneath a cluster of leaves. "Come look," he called. "Strawberries!"

Sure enough, there was a patch of strawberries at the back of the house, just waiting to be picked. There were raspberries too, and huckleberries, and a row of small trees with cherries just ripening.

"It's a real orchard," Mrs. Stafford said. "Fruit of every kind. And it looks like there's an old vegetable garden too."

As fast as he could John was picking berries

and cramming them into his mouth. "Mmm, they're good. The best I ever tasted."

Then a question came into his mind. Had any other boys ever picked fruit from this patch? Maybe the log mansion held the answer.

"I'm going inside." He disappeared around the side of the house.

"I'm coming with you!" Linda cried, dashing up behind.

When they got to the front of the building, they stopped running. Slowly, and a little nervously, they approached the heavy front doors.

"Wouldn't it be funny," Linda whispered, "if the door opened by itself and a witch popped out!"

"There's no such thing as witches." John spoke firmly, but he held his breath as he pulled the door open. With his heart beating fast, he stepped into a huge front room made of peeled cedar logs.

There was an enormous stone fireplace, big enough to roast an ox, and a great wooden table fixed into the floor. Otherwise, except for cobwebs, the room was quite empty. A strange stillness hung in the air. John jumped when he heard his father's voice behind him.

"What a great place!" Mr. Stafford ran his

13

hand along the walls. "These logs were hand cut — you can tell by their roughness. And look at this floor. It's been laid shipdeck fashion, like a ballroom. There must have been some big parties here at one time. That raised platform at the other end is where the orchestra would have been."

Everyone looked at the platform, trying to imagine the orchestra and the people who had danced to its music long ago. They tiptoed across the floor and peeped into the old-fashioned kitchen. There was no one to tell them to be quiet, but somehow the room had the air of a cathedral.

Softly they walked up the winding staircase and poked their noses into all the bedrooms. Nothing but dust and cobwebs. Nowhere was there any trace of the previous occupants whose happy music must once have filled the mansion. Why had they left it, empty and forlorn, like a ghost from the past?

All the bedrooms had doors leading to the high, railed balcony. Stepping out onto it, the Staffords saw the whole island spread out in front of them.

"Oh boy!" John sucked in his breath. This was the most exciting place he had ever seen. There were tall trees to climb and winding

14

trails to explore and a gurgling stream to fish in. There were rocks and cliffs — maybe with caves, John thought. And on the other side of the hill there was a stretch of golden sand.

"A beach! Look, John, there's a beach." Ricky's high-pitched voice broke the stillness. "Let's go to it quick," he squealed.

Before anyone could stop him, he had streaked across the bedroom and down the stairs. Hearing the heavy front door slam, the rest of the family rushed after him. It seemed as though only a minute had elapsed, but when they reached the outside, Ricky was nowhere to be seen.

"Rick, where are you?" Mrs. Stafford called.

From the woods that ringed the house came his excited answer, "I'm here, and I've found some little houses. Come and see."

As they headed toward the woods, Rick came to meet them. He pointed toward a group of five small log cabins, and he looked as proud and important as if he had built them himself.

"Ricky, you must never run off like that. You should stay with the rest of us," his father scolded, firmly taking Ricky's hand.

They went to look at the cabins, which were just as empty as the big house. John looked around carefully, poking into corners, searching for some clue. Then, walking around to the back, he gave a shout. "Here's another place, and this one's different!"

He was staring at a house that was set apart from the others. It was built on a solid foundation and looked like a real family dwelling. Inside they found a big living room, a kitchen, and three bedrooms upstairs.

"This has been modernized." Mr. Stafford gazed around with keen eyes. "Look at the wiring and the plumbing. Someone started to work on it and then stopped. I wonder why?"

He inspected the whole house and shook his head in bewilderment. "It's very strange. Why was all this left empty? It's an ideal spot for a holiday resort. Everything's here. It wouldn't require much work to bring it up to date. I can't imagine why no one has done it."

"Why don't *we* do it?" The words burst from John's mouth before he realized it. "We could live in this house and make the big place into a hotel. The little ones could be guest cabins."

He caught his father's arm in excitement. "We could do it, Dad. You know all about building, and Mom could fix the garden. Then we'd write to our friends back home and they could all come here for their vacations —"

"You've got it all figured out, haven't you?"

His father laughed. "I'm afraid it wouldn't be quite as easy as you think. There would be a lot of problems to deal with first."

"Well, we'd have to solve the mystery, of course, but we could do that —"

"What we're going to do right now, John, is try to find that beach we saw from the balcony. Let's forget about mysteries for a while."

But John couldn't forget. As he followed his father along the moss-covered trail, he wondered why parents always wanted you to forget the most interesting things. They liked everything to be easy and straightforward, and they didn't seem to understand that mysteries could be the most fun.

If he could only stay here, he was sure he could solve the mystery of the empty log houses and learn why the island was deserted and neglected.

"Hey, John, hurry up. It's wonderful here."

John blinked as Linda's voice came to him suddenly. While he had been standing in one spot daydreaming, the others had reached the beach. Now he raced down the hill, kicking off his sneakers as he went.

As Linda had said, the beach was indeed wonderful. It was wide and circular, sheltered by high cliffs on each side and full of all kinds

17

of interesting objects washed up by the tide. There were pieces of driftwood that had broken loose from logs being towed up and down the coast, and lengths of chain and rope that had been used to hold the logs together. And there were dozens of little rock pools of shallow water, teeming with marine life.

Ricky poked his finger at the tiny crabs, then laughed delightedly as they scuttled away to safety. Linda stared in fascination at the brightly colored starfish clinging to the rocks, the sea anemones in emerald, amethyst and gold, and the jellyfish, opening and shutting like tiny umbrellas.

"Isn't this terrific," she exclaimed. "I've never seen anything like it before."

"You won't see anything like it in many places these days," Mrs. Stafford murmured, gazing into one of the pools. "So much of our seashore has become polluted that these beautiful little creatures are disappearing."

"But there's no pollution in this marvelous place," Mr. Stafford declared.

When John saw his father smile and take a deep breath of the pure air, he seized his opportunity. "So why can't we live here and make sure it doesn't get polluted?"

He rushed on hurriedly, before anyone could answer. "We have to live somewhere

18

and Dad has to find some work to do, so why can't we live here and make a holiday resort? What's the good of leaving our friends and coming to a different part of the country if we're going to live in an ordinary place and do ordinary things? We could have real adventures here!"

"We'd help with the work," Linda chimed in eagerly.

Ricky, catching the excitement, came running from the water's edge where he had been collecting sand dollars. "Can we live here?" he asked. "Can this be my beach?"

"My goodness, I seem to be surrounded." Mr. Stafford put his hands out as though for protection. "I'd like to live here too," he said, "but I don't know if we can. I don't know if we can afford a whole island. It might cost an awful lot of money. Besides, I don't even know if it's for sale, or why those buildings are all empty and neglected.

"But I promise you one thing . . ." He paused and John waited with bated breath. "Tomorrow we'll make inquiries and see what we can find out."

Lost Gold and
Hidden Treasure

As it happened, the Staffords began to find out about the island the very same day. When they returned to the motel, the boat-rental man greeted them with a friendly smile. "Well, did you enjoy yourselves?" he asked.

"We found a little island and it's going to be *our* island, even the beach." Ricky was bursting with the news. "We're going to live in one of the log houses. There's six little ones and one great huge one that John calls a mansion."

"That sounds like Disaster Island." The rental man's smile had gone. "All the nice, well-kept islands around here, and your first day out you happen on that awful place."

John and Linda exchanged a glance. It was just like a grown-up to think a "nice, well-kept" place was better than a wild, exciting one. John hoped his parents wouldn't listen, but his father was already asking a question.

"What was the name you called it?"

"Disaster Island. It's not the real name, I guess, but that's how everyone around here knows it. And they steer clear of it, I can tell you. Too many queer things have happened there."

"What kinds of things?" Mr. Stafford asked. "Can you name a few?"

"Well, I can't exactly name them." The rental man scratched his head. "I only know I hear lots of talk. Maybe Len can tell you more."

He called to a young man just getting out of the water and introduced him as Leonard Greaves. "Len really knows this coast. He's helping with the boat rentals today, but mostly he's swimming or diving or sailing somewhere. What was it you were saying about Disaster Island, Len?"

Leonard Greaves answered quickly. "Disaster Island? Keep far away from it. That's the best advice I can give you. Everyone who's had anything to do with that place has landed in bad trouble. If I were you, sir —"

21

"We like it." John couldn't keep quiet a minute longer. He didn't trust this Leonard Greaves. His mouth smiled, but his eyes darted around without looking directly at anyone. "We're going to find out about it tomorrow, aren't we, Dad?"

"Yes, we're going into Victoria to make inquiries. If anyone can tell me some facts, I'll listen. But I'm not interested in rumors and superstitions. Besides, if no one else wants the island, maybe the price won't be too high."

John squeezed his father's arm happily. Thank goodness Dad didn't listen to Leonard Greaves' kind of talk. He believed in making up his own mind.

But his father also believed in asking questions to help him make up his mind, and the trouble was that everyone said the same kinds of things Leonard Greaves did.

The lady who sold picture postcards turned pale at the mention of the name. "I'd never set foot on the place. I hear it's haunted."

"No, I've never been there." The waitress who served their dinner shook her head. "I'd be too scared to go. I hear there's a curse on that island."

The motel manager felt the same way. He was sure there was something wrong with the island, though he didn't know what.

Leonard Greaves came toward them as they left the motel the next morning to catch the bus for Victoria. John was afraid he was going to talk against the island again, but he just handed Mr. Stafford a business card with the words "Harry Abbott, Real Estate" printed on it, and underneath, "Specializing in Island Property."

"The office is just across the street from the bus station," Leonard Greaves said. "You'll be able to find out everything you want to know from Harry Abbott."

John didn't want to find out anything from any friend of Leonard Greaves, but his father said that since they had to pass the office, they might as well go in.

Harry Abbott was a short, heavy man with bushy eyebrows. It seemed to John, who was watching him closely, that a strange expression came over his face when he heard that Len Greaves had given them his name.

"Oh, yes. You're the people who were at Disaster Island."

How did he know? John wondered. Had Leonard Greaves phoned and told him? — and if so, why?

"That island is not for sale," Mr. Abbott said. "The owner died and his family are all out of the country. However" — a big smile

23

spread across his face — "I can show you lots of other island properties, fully developed and better value in every way than that neglected, overgrown place. I'd be happy to take you for a cruise so you can see them all."

John leaned toward his dad and caught his arm urgently. "No," he hissed. "Please, Dad, no." Who wanted some plain old property in some other place? Probably something safe and dull, where there would never be any adventure.

He sighed with relief when his father said, "No, thank you, not today."

When they were outside in the street, he burst out: "I think it's a plot. I think there's something funny going on."

"Now, John, you're letting your imagination run away with you again." Mrs. Stafford spoke reprovingly. "I know you fell in love with the island. All of us felt the same way. But if it's not for sale, we'll just have to be sensible and look for something else."

Sensible! John didn't want to be sensible. He wanted that deserted island, and he didn't believe Harry Abbott for a minute. He turned to Linda with a look that said "Help!" Quickly Linda broke into the conversation.

"Aren't those the government buildings

across the road, Mom? Wouldn't we be able to get some real information there?"

"Sure we would, and they'll have a library with old maps and newspapers. Let's try it."

John grabbed Linda's hand and murmured, "Thanks. That was quick thinking." The two of them raced across the street, running through the gardens toward the statue of Queen Victoria and up the steps to the rotunda, where John ran right into an elderly gentleman, almost knocking him down.

"Oh gosh, I'm sorry. Are you all right?"

He waited till the white-haired man assured him that he was unhurt, then he was off again, running into the building and up the stairs.

There were so many halls and rooms that he and Linda got lost a few times, but at last they found their way to the Legislative Library — where a new disappointment awaited them. A group of visitors was being shown around the handsome old building, and the library was full to overflowing.

"I guess we'll have to come back later," Linda said.

But John was afraid to wait for fear his parents would give up on the island and look for another place. He squeezed through the doorway, making his way toward one of the guides.

In his rush he banged into the edge of a table, knocking some maps to the floor.

"Sorry." He bent down to pick up the maps, and his face turned red as he found himself looking into the bright blue eyes of the same white-haired gentleman he had bumped into before.

"Sorry to be so clumsy." He forced himself to move more slowly and carefully, and he spoke to the guide in his most polite voice.

"Excuse me. Could you give us some information about a small deserted island in the Strait of Georgia? It has a big log house on it."

The guide looked flustered. "I can't help you just now, but maybe Captain Sam could tell you something. He likes talking to people, and he's in the library here almost every day looking through old maps and things. He'd have more information than I have anyway."

She beckoned to someone, and once again John's face grew hot as he saw the elderly gentleman with the white hair and blue eyes heading toward them.

"Captain Samuel Mulholland, late of the coastal service." The old man introduced himself and winked at John in a friendly way. Then he shook hands with Mr. and Mrs. Stafford, who had now caught up. "If there is any information I can give you," he said, "please don't hesitate to ask. My greatest pleasure is to talk to visitors about the history of this coast."

Mr. Stafford explained about the island and the captain listened intently.

"So you stumbled onto that old place." His voice had turned soft, almost dreamy. "No one goes there any more, but once upon a time — oh, I remember how beautiful it was. The Spanish explorers called it Bella, which means beautiful, then later it was shortened to Bell — Bell Island. That's how it appears on the old maps."

John could feel himself relax. New hope began to flow through him. Here at last was someone who knew the island and sounded as though he liked it. He gazed at Captain Mulholland, listening carefully, and the captain smiled at him.

"I wasn't as old as you, young man, when I heard of the Cariboo gold miner who was shipwrecked off Bell Island."

"A shipwrecked gold miner?" Linda's voice rose to a squeak, and the captain's smile grew wider. He led the way to a quiet bench in the hall outside the library and beckoned to the others.

"It was the year 1861," he began, "and the

man's name was James Gregor, a mean and suspicious character, by all accounts. He had struck it rich on the Fraser River and was returning to Victoria with his gold. But James Gregor didn't trust his fellow man. He lived in fear of his gold being stolen, and instead of crossing the Strait of Georgia in the paddle-wheeler with the other men, he set sail on his own. His body was found on a rock at Bell Island. But" — the captain paused dramatically — "the gold he had given his life to save was never found."

Linda asked breathlessly, "You mean it's still there? No one has found it after all these years?"

"Lots of people have searched for it, but so far it has never been found."

Maybe I could find it! The exciting thought flashed into John's mind. The scene around him faded away, and instead he saw himself digging outside the log mansion. He saw the shining flash of gold nuggets the size of a man's fist.

He came back to the present with a start as Ricky, growing bored with all the talk, began to tug at his arm.

"Quiet, Rick." He held his young brother firmly and turned back toward the captain, determined not to miss a word.

"Apart from gold prospectors," Captain Mulholland went on, "no one actually lived on the island until 1908, when it was bought by a European prince."

"Wow, a prince!" Linda cried. This was getting better all the time.

"All kinds of rich and titled Europeans were interested in this part of the world around that time, and many built summer homes here. The prince built a great chateau, made from the finest cedar in the Northwest, each log chosen separately and peeled by hand.

"Every summer he arrived with his staff, who lived in the small cabins, and he gave wonderful parties to which he invited important people from all over the world. There were always some people from Victoria, and one summer I worked on the boat that took guests over to the island."

The captain's eyes twinkled. "I was supposed to stay on the boat, but being young and curious, I sneaked off to peek through the windows of the big house. And what a sight it was! The beautiful room was decorated with tapestries and paintings — all kinds of art treasures such as I had never seen before.

"The ladies wore flashing jewels in their hair and the gentlemen were in formal evening wear. As for the dinner, there were so

29

many dishes it would have made you dizzy. An orchestra was playing and the guests waltzed around the floor, with the prince leading the Grand Promenade."

John leaned forward eagerly. "What happened to the prince?" he asked. "Why did he go away and leave everything?"

"The First World War came along, my boy. The prince was called to his regiment. Six months later he was dead — and when news of his death was reported in the papers, looters swarmed over to the island and stripped the chateau of all its beautiful furnishings.

"The prince had a caretaker named Lee Jang, who lived on the island year round. It was said that he managed to hide some of the art treasures. But Lee himself died soon after the prince, so no one ever discovered what happened. If anything was saved, it has never been found."

He paused, and for a moment there was silence. Captain Mulholland seemed far away. Finally, with a sigh, he finished his story.

"After that, several people tried different business ventures on the island, but none ever succeeded. Everything got run down and people started calling it Disaster Island. It was a foolish name for such a lovely place, but like many foolish names, it stuck."

John couldn't hold the words back another minute. "But all that was such a long time ago! Why do people today keep saying it's a bad place? We want to live on the island and make it into a resort, but people keep warning us against it, and that real estate man says it's not for sale."

"John thinks it's a plot," Linda put in. "He doesn't believe Harry Abbott or the things people say."

"Neither do I," the captain said. "It sounds as though someone is purposely spreading rumors to keep people away. There's a mystery there somewhere."

He looked at the Staffords with his bright blue eyes. "You're sure you want to go ahead with your plans? It might be very difficult. These people who are spreading the rumors might make trouble for you. Are you still sure it's what you want?"

"Yes," John said.

"Yes," Linda echoed.

"Yes," Ricky warbled in his squeaky voice.

Mr. and Mrs. Stafford were silent for a moment, and John held his breath.

"Yes," Mr. Stafford said firmly. "I'm not looking for any trouble, but I'm not going to give in either. This is a free country, and if I

31

want to live some place, I'm not going to let any rumor mongers stop me."

"I feel the same way," Mrs. Stafford agreed.

"Good." Captain Mulholland looked pleased. "You've got me really interested now. I'm going to look through my old files and see what I can find out. I'd sure like to see that island made beautiful again."

He turned to John, whispering in his ear. "I think, my boy, you're going to have a lot of investigating and mystery solving to do before you crack this one."

"But I'll do it in the end." John's eyes were gleaming. A dozen ideas were whirling through his mind and he could already see himself solving the mystery and finding the lost gold and treasure. He could hardly wait to start.

Tracks in the Sand

John rolled over and reached for the alarm, but it wasn't the alarm. Who could be calling at this hour of the morning? he thought, stumbling out of bed and over to the telephone. As he listened to the voice at the other end of the line, a delighted grin spread across his face.

"Dad, Captain Sam wants to speak to you," he said, putting down the receiver and gently waking his father.

"I knew it," said John, sitting down on the edge of Linda's bed as their father answered the phone.

"Knew what?" mumbled Linda.

"I just knew it," he repeated mysteriously. He wanted her to be awake when she heard what he had to say.

"Tell me!" she said, sitting straight up, her eyes blazing with curiosity.

"Linda," John whispered, "something queer really *is* going on. It wasn't just my imagination! Captain Sam phoned. He's been investigating and he's found that Harry Abbott was lying about the island not being for sale. The owners are out of the country, but a lawyer in Vancouver has been left in charge. Dad's talking to Captain Sam about it now."

After Mr. Stafford heard Captain Sam's story, he put in a call to the lawyer and made an appointment. An hour later he and Mrs. Stafford were on the ferry to Vancouver.

Back at the motel, John didn't say anything to Linda and Rick, but he was worried. How could they be sure that this lawyer in Vancouver wasn't in the plot too? He could pretend that he wanted to sell and then set the price sky high or make impossible terms that the Staffords would never be able to meet.

John wished he could have gone along to size up the situation. His parents were just too trusting. But he had to stay behind and wait, and all day he was restless, looking at the clock a thousand times, counting the minutes until his parents got back. Yet when he finally saw them walking up the path, he couldn't move. He wanted desperately to hear the news but at the same time was afraid to hear it.

Finally it was Linda who shouted, "What happened? Tell us quick!"

Then John saw that his parents were beaming, and his mother was waving a legal-looking document. "It's all settled," she called, and he let out his breath at last, jumping in the air with a loud whoop.

"There'll be a lot of work to do." Mr. Stafford was looking serious now. "By the time we've bought everything we need to fix up the place, most of our savings will be used up. We'll have no money for help, so we'll all have to pitch in."

"Oh, we will, we will!" John couldn't get the words out fast enough. What did hard work matter when it meant living on that exciting island? As for being short of money, there was all that lost gold and treasure just waiting to be found.

But there were also those people who had been trying to keep them away from the island. That evening, when the family visited Captain Sam to discuss their new home, John tried to find out more about them. While the others looked at the captain's compasses and sextants, John drew him aside and asked him in a low voice, "What do you think they'll do when they find out we're there?"

He didn't say who or where, but Captain Sam understood. "You'd better keep your eyes and ears open, John." He spoke in the same low voice. "Stay on your guard and keep looking and listening for anything suspicious."

John would have liked to start looking and listening right away, but there was lots to be done before they could move to the island. The first problem was where to live while they were fixing the old Lee Jang house, which would be their future home.

"How about a floathouse?" Captain Sam suggested. "It's like a boathouse. It's a wooden cabin on the water, anchored to a log boom or a wharf. You can get a used one at a reasonable price, and then you can imagine you're in one of the logging camps upcoast where whole communities live on the water that way."

"Wow, that sounds really neat." John's eyes were shining. "Wait till the kids back home hear about this!"

He could hardly wait to see what a floathouse really looked like, and all his expectations were satisfied when they went to look at one the next day. The man at the wharf took them into a compact little house sitting squarely on its platform of logs. It was fitted with bunks, a table that folded against the wall and a stove with a pipe through the roof. The big "For Sale" sign was pulled off as soon as Mr. and Mrs. Stafford completed the deal.

Next came the excitement of choosing a boat, which would be their transportation instead of a car. They finally settled on a rugged-looking motorboat. The captain gave John and Linda lessons in handling it so they could go on errands to the larger islands to pick up mail and groceries.

"There's one thing I want you to remember," he said. "Always use the wharf, never the beach — not unless you want to end up like James Gregor. The beach itself is safe, but the approaches to it are full of submerged rocks and dangerous reefs that can tear a boat to pieces."

"Why don't they build a lighthouse there?" Ricky piped up.

"Because it's out of the main shipping lines," the captain explained. "No one goes that way unless they're heading for the island, and only an experienced navigator who knows those waters would ever try it. Now" — he turned to Linda and John — "I want you to promise that you'll always keep away from that area in the boat."

"I promise," Linda said promptly.

"Me too," John said. He didn't know that the time would come when he would wish he'd never made that promise.

But just then he wasn't paying much attention to the captain's warning. He was excited because tomorrow they were going out to the island to work for the day. Their first project was to get rid of the rotten wood on the old wharf and make it safe again, then to attach a floating dock between the still sturdy pilings in the water to make a bigger docking area to unload supplies and receive their guests when they started to come. After that they had to clear the overgrown path between the landing and the house they'd be fixing. When these jobs were done they'd be ready for the lumber and supplies.

Since Mom still had some shopping to do, Captain Sam came along in her place. He knew exactly where to go, and in spite of the float they were towing along behind, it didn't take long to reach the island. John, leaning forward eagerly, caught a glimpse of it as the boat rounded the point; it looked just as mysterious, just as much an adventure island, as when he had seen it for the first time.

When they arrived, John jumped out and tied the boat up. He scanned the shore for any

38

suspicious signs, but there was no time for investigating. Mr. Stafford and Captain Sam had brought hammers and saws, and there was work for everyone.

They began with the mending of the wharf. Though most of the wood at the outer end was decayed and crumbling, much of that near the shore was still good. As the men tore off the old wood, John and Linda and Ricky carted it away. Before long, with the addition of a bit of new lumber and some strong spikes, the remaining structure was sound — and safe.

Next came the maneuvering of the float into place.

"Let us do it," Linda begged. "We have our bathing suits — let us put it in."

Her father agreed, and Linda and John took off their jeans and slipped into the water, ignoring the rocks underfoot. With John pulling the tow rope and Linda pushing and steering, the dock moved slowly but easily between the pilings. Then Mr. Stafford and Captain Sam chained it firmly to the end of the wharf.

"Now let's rest a minute, then the captain and I are going to start cutting down the brush," Mr. Stafford announced when the dock was in place. "I want you three to take the cuttings out of the way so we can have a clear path. You can put them with that old wood, and one day we'll have a big bonfire."

But John was too excited to rest. As soon as he had dressed again he called, "Let's have a race. Let's see who can take away the most cuttings."

Enthusiastically they started to work again. But this job was harder than they had expected. The sun beat down on their heads, the rough branches scratched their hands, and the stooping made their backs ache. They were all very glad when their father told them to take a break.

"You can go off for a while," he said, "but don't stray too far. There's a storm warning out, so we won't be staying much longer. I want you to come back and finish the job as soon as you hear me blow the boat horn. Okay?"

"Okay," they chorused, racing off as though shot from a catapult. But near the mansion they all slowed down. Even though they knew what to expect this time, they still had a quivery feeling as they gazed at the building.

The heavy door swung open under their touch, and once more they stood in the great hall. The captain's story sounded in their ears, and out of the shadows they seemed to see a colorful scene from the past. On the raised platform an orchestra played a waltz; and on the polished floor elegantly dressed guests were dancing gracefully.

John could see chefs in tall white hats bringing in festive dishes, one after the other. Linda saw Oriental attendants opening the doors to admit a group of naval officers, quite dashing in their blue capes lined with white satin and fastened with gold chains.

It all seemed so real that they jumped when they heard a very modern sound — a news broadcast. Their father stood in the doorway, a transistor radio in his hand. He too was looking around the bare room with dreams in his eyes.

"One day," he said softly, "I hope we can bring this place to life again. I hope we can fill it with light and music and happy vacationers.

"By the way," he added, as he brushed a few cobwebs from the broad window sill, "I came to tell you that you can go to the beach if you like. The weather forecast has changed. There's no more storm warning, so we don't have to rush away yet. Just make sure you come back to the wharf as soon as you hear me blowing the boat horn."

Delightedly they assured him that they would come when they heard the signal. They were so eager to get to the beach that they were out the door and down the steps before they realized that Ricky was no longer with them.

"Where's he got to this time?" John groaned as he looked around. "That kid can't stay in one place for more than a minute."

"Maybe he's in one of the little houses. Let's look."

But Rick wasn't in any of the little houses, or in the bigger one where Lee Jang had lived. He wasn't in any of the rooms in the mansion, or in the overgrown gardens, front or back. Nowhere could they find any sign of the inquisitive little boy. Then, just as they were beginning to get really worried, they heard a small sound and discovered Rick standing right behind them. They both pounced on him.

"Where were you?"

"Why didn't you answer when we called?"

"You know Mom told you not to go off on your own."

"How did you get here without us seeing you?"

Ricky looked from one to the other with a mischievous smile. "I found a secret hiding place."

"A secret hiding place?"

42

Another time John would have laughed, but just now he was interested in secret places. When you were searching for lost treasure you had to investigate any possible clue, even if it came from Ricky.

"Where is your hiding place?" he asked. "How about showing it to Lin and me?"

The little boy shook his head. "It's *my* place. I'm not going to show it to anyone."

"All right, then, keep it to yourself." John knew that the more he asked, the more obstinate Ricky would become. It probably wasn't much of a place anyway, and he'd find it himself without any help.

"You'd better not run off again, though," he warned, "or I'll take you right back to Dad and you won't be able to come to the beach with us."

With such a threat hanging over his head, Ricky was very quiet until they reached the beach. Then he sat down in the water fully dressed and happily began to play.

Linda gazed at the peaceful expanse of smooth water under the clear sky. Then she imagined it wind-whipped and churning, as it must have been the night James Gregor was lost.

"I wonder what happened to the gold," she mused.

43

John looked at the tall cliffs on either side of the bay. "There must be some caves or holes in the rocks, and I'm going to investigate them all. I'm going to search each one from top to bottom — starting right now."

He pulled off his sneakers and socks and rolled up his jeans. But just as he was stepping into the water, he suddenly gasped and pointed a shaking finger toward the shoreline. "Look! There's been a boat here. You can see the marks where it was beached."

Linda slid down beside him, her voice a breathless whisper. "Remember what Captain Sam said about no one coming this way unless they were heading for this island?"

"And only an experienced navigator who knows these waters would ever attempt it."

They stared at each other wide-eyed. Then, turning again to look at the marks in the sand, they saw something even more incredible.

Behind the boat mark was a huge footprint, bigger than anything they had ever seen before. Neither Leonard Greaves nor Harry Abbott had feet that size, so someone else must have been here last night — someone who left monstrous prints when he walked.

◆

Day of Discovery

"Let's go over what we know so far." John was acting very businesslike, turning his back on that enormous footprint. "We know there's some kind of plot to keep everyone away from this island. We think there's a group of people in the plot but we don't know who they are, or why they're doing these things."

Linda was gazing at the boat marks. "Maybe . . ." she said slowly, "maybe they want to keep everyone away so they can come here themselves and no one will know they're here."

"That's an idea." John jumped up excitedly. "It would mean they're probably doing something that's against the law."

Linda nodded. "Maybe they're smugglers. Remember Captain Sam told us about the rum runners on this coast in the old days?"

"Or maybe they're spies. We're very close to the border."

John looked across the water at the tall peaks of the Olympic Peninsula in the State of Washington. But instead of the mountains he was seeing newspaper headlines: *John and Linda Stafford break international spy ring! Master Spy Bigfoot captured at last!*

He was brought back to the present by the sound of the boat horn from the dock.

Linda stood up right away. "Come on, John. We promised to do our share of the work and we've got to go now." She took Ricky's hand and started up the path. But John had to have one more look at the boat mark and the footprint. The other two had reached the top before he grabbed his sneakers and came racing after them.

In his hurry he forgot about his socks lying on the sand. Halfway back to the boat he remembered them. "Oh well," he thought, "they'll give me an excuse to go back and investigate on my own next time."

Next time was three days later, when the whole Stafford family arrived to take possession of their island. The floathouse was tied up at the wharf, and everyone was inside, enjoying the novelty of this new home on the water. Suddenly John asked if he could go to the beach to find his socks.

"You want to go now?" His mother seemed surprised that he should want to leave this exciting new dwelling to look for something like socks. But when John nodded she said he could go, and he was off before anyone could ask to go with him.

This time he searched the beach very thoroughly, but though he examined everywhere with great care, he could find no signs of an intruder. No more boat marks, no footprints, nothing. Yet someone had been here a few nights ago — someone who had braved the dangerous rocks in the dark — and maybe that person would return.

"What I need," John thought to himself, "is a place where I can keep watch and see anyone heading this way."

The balcony on the mansion provided a good view of the island, but not of the water surrounding it. For this he would need higher ground. It seemed to John that the last time he was on the balcony he had noticed a rocky point that looked as though it might make a lookout. What he had to do now was find it.

He was still thinking about a lookout when he arrived back at the floathouse and found the rest of the family making plans for the best way to spend the day.

"Why don't we explore the whole island today," John said. "There's still lots of it we haven't seen, and tomorrow the building supplies will be coming and we'll be busy."

"So let's explore today, and let's start right now." Linda was already at the door, but John beckoned her to wait.

"I've got another idea. Suppose we divide the island into different sections and each of us explore a section of our own, then report to the others. We could go to the balcony first to look around and choose the section we want." *And I could find the place to build my lookout*, he thought to himself.

"Terrific!" Linda shot out the door, racing toward the mansion, with John and Ricky close behind. When they arrived, they all trooped upstairs to the balcony. One glance told John which part he wanted to explore. He pointed to a rocky peak that stood out above the rest. "That's where I'd like to go."

They all set off in different directions. The familiar path to the beach led south and Ricky ran toward it, with his parents following him at a slower pace. Linda headed in a westerly direction, and John turned north into a stand of tall hemlocks and dogwoods.

48

His footsteps made no sound on the thick carpet of moss. Alone now, he was able to look around and observe all the sights and sounds of the forest. He saw a doe step out from behind a tree, her big ears flicking. He watched a grouse drumming on an old stump and laughed at a pair of chipmunks playing a lively game of tag. Then the trees began to thin and he heard the musical tinkle of running water.

Heading toward the sound, he found himself in a broad green meadow with a stream, like a flash of silver, winding along one edge. The grass was springy, the ground flat and smooth.

"A baseball field," John gasped. "It would be just perfect for that." He began to run, curving his arm as though to pitch, startling a family of jack rabbits who stared at him in surprise.

What a fabulous island this was, what an absolutely wonderful place, John thought. It had *everything*, including a potential ball park. Already he was planning to invite a group of kids to play ball — he had seen lots of them on the islands they had passed — and when the game was over they could run into the stream for a cooling dip.

John gave a sigh of contentment. Next summer, when they had things fixed up, there would be happy vacationers to share this marvelous place with him. It was his home now — and no one was going to take it away from him.

"No one." He spoke the words aloud, with determination. He thought of the marks on the beach and the lookout he had set out to find, and he jumped to his feet. At the far end of the field the terrain began to change, becoming rocky and steep. Maybe the lookout he was searching for would be that way.

Quickly he began climbing. Soon he was hot and panting, but he finally arrived at the top on a craggy plateau. Breathlessly he looked around, then groaned with disappointment. Though he could see the whole island from here, he still couldn't see the water surrounding it; and it was the approaches he would need to watch if he was to check on any intruders.

How could he keep watch without a proper lookout? As far as he knew, this was the highest point on the island, and still it wasn't high enough. Then he noticed the twisted arbutus tree that stood in the middle of the plateau — the only tree growing among the rocks.

It was not very large but it was sturdy. John hauled himself up the trunk, finding footholds and handholds in the twisted wood. He found a strong limb to sit on, and then he gave a shout of triumph. This was it. This was the view he had been wanting. With the extra height, he could now see all the approaches to the island for a long way around.

He could see the Gulf Islands to the north, Saturna, Pender, Galiano and the others. To the west was Haro Strait and the southern part of Vancouver Island. If he had had the binoculars, he might even have been able to see Victoria. The east was very clear. He could see right across the water to the Washington mainland, where Mount Baker raised its snowy head above the clouds. To the south, past the beach, the Olympic mountains shone in the sun.

The branch made an uncomfortable seat, but John figured that he could build a sort of platform, like a tree house. Then he would be able to spend hours here keeping guard, and no one coming to the island from any direction would be able to escape his eagle eye.

Quickly he scrambled down from the tree. He had been in a hurry to find this place. Now he was in just as big a hurry to find out if he could have some lumber to build a platform. He would have to be careful, of course, not to give away the real reason why he wanted a lookout. He and Linda had agreed not to worry their parents with their suspicions. They were going to investigate and solve the mystery on their own.

John was thinking about this as he walked toward the floathouse, but Ricky's high-pitched voice broke into his thoughts. His young brother came running toward him, holding out a shiny green glass ball.

"Look what I found, John! It's a Japanese fishing float, Mom says, and it came to our beach all the way from Japan."

"Well, maybe not all the way from Japan." Mrs. Stafford laughed. "But it did come from a Japanese fishing boat."

She stopped as Linda too came rushing toward them, waving something in the air. She was breathless with excitement, and when John saw what she was holding in her hand, he cried, "Wow! Indian relics! A spearhead and an old stone pestle. They're just like the ones in the museum!"

"And I found them right on our own land." Linda's voice was awed. "Maybe there was an Indian fishing village here at one time."

Everyone was silent for a moment, imagining the Indians who might have beached their dugout canoes on this island after a fishing expedition.

Linda looked dreamy-eyed. "One day I'm going to do some real digging in the same spot and see what other Indian things I can find." She turned to John. "What about you, Oh-Unusually-Silent-One? Didn't you find anything?"

John told them about the stream and the smooth green field that would make such a super ball park. He told about the view from the arbutus tree and his plans for building a treehouse, though he didn't mention the real reason why he wanted it. He grinned with pleasure when his father said he could have all the lumber he wanted. Everything was going right today. No problems, no worries — only good things happening.

In fact, John felt so good that he let down his guard and forgot about watching and listening for anything suspicious.

Full of high spirits, he ran down to the beach with the others. While floating lazily in the clear water, he planned the construction of his lookout. Later he and Linda went clam digging, raking in a whole pailful of small butter clams. Then, hungry as always, John built a fire near a rock and steamed the clams for the family's supper.

Finally, when no one could manage another bite, Mr. and Mrs. Stafford got up and headed slowly back to the floathouse with Ricky. John and Linda stayed behind and sat gazing into the fire, watching the colored flames that driftwood always makes.

The sun had gone down and the sky was darkening. With a flash of phosphorescence a salmon rose to the light cast by the fire, and a seal surfaced with a loud snort.

"Isn't this just the greatest place? Isn't it just absolutely perfect?" Looking around with a sigh of contentment, John had no thought in his mind of the giant footprint or the rumors that people were spreading about the island.

When his father called "Bedtime," he didn't even argue. He and Linda doused the fire and went back to the cozy floathouse. John snuggled into his bunk and fell asleep to the soft creaking of the floating dock as it moved on its chains with the tide.

Then suddenly he was awake, sitting up in bed. The sun was just rising. It wasn't time to get up yet. What was it that had wakened him? Everything seemed peaceful inside, and outside was calm and quiet.

Quiet! The thought hit him with a jolt, and it was then that he realized why it was so still. The creaking of the dock had stopped.

He slipped out of bed, padding silently to

the door and closing it behind him. Then he stood there staring incredulously at the end of the wharf.

The dock was gone! It was nowhere in sight, and only the pilings showed where it once had been.

A Mysterious Disappearance

What could have happened to it? There had been no storm last night, no strong winds that could have sunk the dock or caused it to break off and drift away. So why had it suddenly disappeared?

Hurriedly John ran out onto the wharf. The thick log pilings were still standing upright. They looked as though they had weathered many storms and could last through many more. But the chains that had fastened the dock to the pilings were gone. The chains had been new, and John remembered how heavy and strong they were. What had happened to them, and to the float, during the night?

"I don't know what to make of it at all," he muttered.

But he knew that a dock was a necessity when you were living on an island, and there was no way they could build another one until the scow arrived from Victoria with the building materials.

"The scow!" John caught his breath sharply. The scow was due to arrive before noon, and now there was no dock from which to unload it.

Was it coincidence that the float had mysteriously vanished just when the scow was coming? Or could it be that someone had found out about it? — someone who didn't want them to have the building supplies, didn't want them to fix up the island. Could that someone be the same person who had left the huge footprint on the beach?

Quickly John looked around to see if anyone was lurking nearby. He stood very still, his eyes roaming the area, his ears tuned for the slightest sound. When he was finally sure he was alone, he began to investigate.

He slipped quietly into the water. The sharp pebbles cut into his bare feet; the cold water of early morning soaked his thin pajamas. But all he could think of was the big gaping space where the dock had been.

Carefully he searched around the pilings, among the barnacles attached to the old wharf, and on the wharf itself. Finding no clue, he began to comb over the rocks on the shore. Suddenly he stopped, staring at a shiny metal object lying on a large rock.

"A chain cutter!"

It was lying there in full view, and as his hand closed around it he knew for sure that his suspicions had been right. Someone had visited the dock last night and snapped the chains with a cutter. It had been deliberately cut from the pilings and set adrift.

Had the evidence been left there deliberately too? It didn't seem likely that whoever had done this would leave a pair of chain cutters out in the open for anyone to see. Not unless he *wanted them to see*, wanted them to know they had an enemy, wanted to scare them away from the island.

"Why didn't I check last night before I went to bed? Why didn't I come down here and check?"

He was so angry with himself that he banged at his forehead with his fists. Then slowly he straightened up. "It won't happen again," he vowed, "and I won't let them get away with this. I'll think of some way to beat them."

But before doing anything else, he ran back to the floathouse and dropped the evidence into his drawer. One day, when he had solved the mystery and outwitted the people who were plotting against them, he would show his parents the chain cutter and tell them the whole story. But just now knowing about the cutter wouldn't help them get the dock back — it would only cause them worry. What with Dad's illness, and all their savings invested in this island, he didn't want to load them with other problems right now.

He couldn't keep the missing float a secret, though. They had to know about that, and as soon as possible.

He bent over his father's sleeping form. "Wake up, Dad. You've got to get up. The dock's gone."

"The what?" Mr. Stafford sat up sleepily. "What's that you said, John? I don't think I heard you right."

"The dock's gone, Dad. It isn't on the pilings any more."

"It isn't on the piles? You must have been dreaming." But Mr. Stafford had to believe it when he raised the window blinds and saw for himself. "My gosh, you're right. It really isn't there!"

Hastily he pulled pants and sweater over

his night clothes, thrust his feet into sneakers and hurried outside. John stripped off his soaking pajamas and quickly put on his jeans.

Linda heard him and woke up as he was heading out the door. It took her no more than a minute to throw on her clothes and follow him. She caught up with him on the wharf and stopped in astonishment.

"What happened?" she asked in an excited whisper. "Was it — *them*? Did whoever it was come again last night?"

John nodded. "The chains were cut and the float pushed out to drift. I found a pair of cutters that must have been used for the job."

"Did you show Dad the cutters?"

"Of course not. What do you take me for?" His whisper was indignant, then it changed, becoming full of dejection. "I don't blame you for not trusting me after the way I muffed things last night. I went to bed without checking the dock. It's partly my fault this happened, because I should have looked."

"It's not your fault at all, John. Even if you had looked you wouldn't have seen anything, because I don't believe anyone was here last night. I was too excited to sleep and I could hear the float creaking away for ages. I bet no one came until a couple of hours ago, so stop blaming yourself. After all, you couldn't have kept guard all night."

"That's what Im going to do tonight. I'm going to sleep outside and keep watch."

"Then I'm going to keep watch with you."

"I thought you would." John couldn't help smiling, though he was still blaming himself inside. "We'll have to plan," he began, then broke off quickly as his father came toward them, looking bewildered.

"I'm darned if I know what happened," Mr. Stafford said. "But maybe the float's just drifting. I'm going to head the boat downwind and look for it offshore. While I'm doing that, I want you two to walk along the shoreline and search for it — just in case it's drifted into one of the coves."

"Okay. We'll start looking right away."

Together John and Linda began their trek along the coast. They crossed the sandy beach and climbed over the rocks to the first cove, their eyes searching all the time. Because the shoreline was jagged, they could see only a short distance ahead. Each time they rounded a curve they looked around hopefully, but no-where was there any sign of the float.

After half an hour of walking, their feet were soaking and their legs were tired. Linda finally called a halt: "When we reach the next point, let's rest for a minute."

"Okay by me," John said. "Maybe we can dry our feet a bit."

But when they rounded the point, they didn't rest. They saw something that made them forget their tiredness.

There, bumping treacherously against a rocky shoal about fifty feet out from the shore, was the dock. It was still in one piece, but every wave that came along pounded it against the rocks with a loud crack. John knew it wouldn't be long before the wood broke apart under such a beating.

"I'd better swim out and try to get it," he said. He looked at the reef and quickly began pulling off his sneakers. "I've got to try and push it off the rocks right away."

Linda shivered as she looked at the water, but she met John's eyes and said with a determined voice, "All right, then, I'm going in too. With those waves tossing it about, you'll never be able to haul it in by yourself."

Linda was a good swimmer and John was glad to have her help — it *would* be hard to push the float off the rocks by himself. "Okay, let's go," he grunted, and together they plunged into the chilling waves and swam out to the shoal.

"Grab hold of this end and I'll swim around to the other —" John's yell broke off with a gasp of pain.

"John! Are you all right?" Linda cried, then watched in dismay as her brother went under. She struck out toward him, but he resurfaced and called to her with a grimace.

"Watch out! There are sharp rocks underwater. I banged my leg into one. It's not bleeding, but it sure hurts!"

Carefully, Linda maneuvered her way back to the dock and grabbed the swaying edge. John finally managed to catch hold of the far end, but by that time a large wave had ripped off one of the planks with a terrific crack. The waves seemed to be getting larger by the minute.

"We've got to get this thing to shore," Linda called. "I can't hold it off the rocks much longer."

"I know! Let's try to push it out a bit from the rocks, then —"

He stopped suddenly, listening. Was that a boat horn he heard? Then Linda was shouting "Dad!" and he saw their father heading toward them in the boat. John had never been so glad to see anyone in his life.

Without asking questions, Mr. Stafford

threw out a tow line. "Run it through the hook at the corner of the float," he yelled.

Linda hung grimly on to her side while John ran the line through at his end and threw the rope to her. She did the same, tossing the end back to her father. Then they both held on while Mr. Stafford pulled the dock safely away from the rocks. As he secured it for towing, they climbed aboard the boat and flopped down thankfully.

Their father stared silently at them for a minute. "You've done a great job and I'm proud of you both," he said, before turning the boat toward home. "Rest for a while now," he added. "I'm afraid there's more work to do when we get back."

Mom and Ricky were waiting for them on the wharf. Ricky was holding a coil of heavy rope and Mrs. Stafford was cutting it into shorter lengths. John and Linda slipped back into the water and carefully maneuvered the float until it rested between the pilings, so that Mr. Stafford could secure the corners with the rope.

"This rope will have to do until we get some new chains, so keep your fingers crossed and hope it will work."

He looped a piece of rope several times around one of the pilings, then threaded it

64

through the ends of the float and knotted it securely. John and Linda each took a piece of rope and did the same thing to two other pilings, and Mr. Stafford nodded approvingly.

"That's got it," he said. "Let's see if it'll hold."

It did. Hanging between the pilings, it moved gently up and down with the waves, making the soft, creaking sound that had suddenly become the most beautiful sound in the world.

"Hooray!" Rick was jumping up and down, and John felt a warm glow of triumph. They had outwitted the plotters, they'd beaten whoever had cut the chains. The thought made him feel wonderful, and as always when he felt good, he was immediately hungry.

"I'm starved," he announced.

His mother smiled. "I knew you would be. There's a big, hot breakfast waiting for you."

John was the first one into the floathouse, rubbing himself dry, changing his clothes, plunking himself hungrily down at the table. Mrs. Stafford kept her promise of a big breakfast, and John and Linda had a contest to see who could eat more of the golden pancakes. They were just clearing away the dishes when they heard a loud whistle. The scow had arrived from Victoria.

65

Everyone crowded to the dock to watch the big, square-bottomed boat pull in. It brought lumber and insulation and fertilizer, and all kinds of supplies to turn the island into a holiday resort.

John sang happily as he helped to unload the equipment. The float was back in place. The building materials had arrived. Everything had turned out well. But just because they had won this battle, he didn't kid himself that they had won the war. Their enemies were probably thinking up some other trick. So John maintained his resolution to sleep outdoors and keep guard.

In the meantime, Mrs. Stafford announced that all plans for work that day were canceled. "Some members of the family have done their share of work already," she said. "I declare the rest of the day a holiday."

Everyone went to the beach for a lazy afternoon and a barbecue supper. Lying on his back, gazing up at the sky, John heard his parents discussing the strange disappearance of the float.

"I still don't understand it," Mr. Stafford said. "I can't see why it should have happened, especially in calm weather. The man in the hardware store assured me that the chain would hold even in a storm. Maybe it had a few bad links. I'll have to ask Sam about it next time we see him."

By then maybe I'll have found out who did it, John thought. He was glad his father wasn't too suspicious; he himself was going to be suspicious of everything and everyone until the mystery was cleared up.

He spoke quietly to Linda. "Tonight's the night to sleep outside. Whoever cut those chains might come poking around again. Are you sure you still want to stay with me?"

"Of course I do!" Linda's eyes were sparkling, and John could feel excitement rising inside him. For the first time in his life he could hardly wait for bedtime.

Dad gave permission right away when John and Linda asked to sleep outdoors. "Just make sure you come inside if it rains," he said. Ricky wanted to sleep out too, but when John promised to let him sleep in the top bunk, he settled for that. Around nine o'clock Mr. and Mrs. Stafford took Ricky into the floathouse, leaving John and Linda alone. John spread out a groundsheet and Linda laid out the sleeping bags.

"You know what worries me," she whispered, "is how we're going to stay awake."

"We'll have to take turns, an hour at a time. I'll take the first turn if you like and you can go to sleep. Then when I get tired, I'll wake you up."

But they were both too excited to be tired. They lay very quietly in their sleeping bags. There was no more talk because even a whisper might give away their whereabouts, and they didn't want an intruder to know they were keeping guard. But though they didn't speak, their eyes searched the darkness.

The night was clear and starlit, and the island echoed with all kinds of sounds. Waves lapped against the shore, trees rustled and the float creaked. A screech owl dropped its bell-like notes into the night, and somewhere on the water a loon gave its melancholy call.

Each time there was a snapping or a stirring, two heads raised noiselessly, but there was never anything to see. Gradually Linda's eyes began to close. John's eyes were feeling heavy too, and when he heard a pebble fall, he didn't move at first. "Probably just a mouse," he thought sleepily. But just to make sure, he raised his head. Then he froze, his eyes glazing over.

On the path that had been empty a few minutes ago, there was now a strange black shadow, so big and so frightening it might have been some prehistoric monster. The feet

were enormous and queerly shaped, the head
was huge, and the back had a kind of hump.
And it was crouched over, as though ready to
spring, just a yard or two from John and
Linda.

The Intruder Returns

John never knew how long he lay there staring; but he must have touched Linda's arm
without knowing it, because she opened her
eyes and sat up. Sleepily she looked around,
then gasped in horror.

"Shhh." John put his hand over her mouth,
but he wasn't quite fast enough. Abruptly the
shadow straightened up. For a moment it
stood very still, while John and Linda held
their breath. Then it turned, lumbered down
the path and disappeared through the trees.

The path was empty now, but still John and
Linda lay huddled in their sleeping bags, not
daring to move. For several minutes, neither
of them could speak. Finally Linda whispered
in a trembling voice, "What was it, John?
What was that awful thing?"

"I don't know," John's voice was a whisper too. "I never saw anything like it before."

He was trying to be calm, but he still shuddered at the thought of that horrible shape. Suppose it had come toward them instead of going away? And what if it returned? What would they do?

The night seemed full of danger now. The sky had darkened, and clouds were gathering blackly overhead. When the first raindrop fell, Linda jumped up with a sigh of relief.

"Dad said we had to go inside if it rained."

She gathered her sleeping bag hurriedly and ran to the floathouse. John followed more slowly. He didn't feel right about deserting his post, but he had promised to come in if it started to rain and if he broke his promise he might not be allowed to sleep outdoors any more.

Quietly they crept into their bunks, pulling the cozy blankets around them. But even now when they were safe and snug, neither of them could sleep. Listening to the rain on the floathouse roof, they kept thinking about the monstrous shadow with the strange hump and the huge head.

"Don't tell anyone what we saw," John whispered to Linda when they got up next morning. His sister nodded gravely. She was

71

as determined as John was that the two of them should solve the mystery on their own without worrying their parents.

"How about tonight? Do you think —" She gulped, trying to swallow her fears. "Do you think we should stay out and watch again?"

John looked through the window at the black clouds. "If this rain keeps on, we won't be allowed to," he said.

The rain did keep on, hour after hour. For a whole week the sky was gray and showery, and there was no chance of sleeping outdoors. Every day John and Linda inspected the path where the shadow had been. They searched the beach for boat marks or footprints and investigated the wharf area very thoroughly. But throughout the week there was no sign of the intruder anywhere.

"Maybe," Linda said, "whatever it is that it comes to do, it can't do in the rain."

"Maybe," John agreed.

But the Stafford family had plenty to do in spite of the rain. There were preserves to make from the fruit they had gathered, and there was the enormous job of making the old Lee Jang house livable before the cold weather came.

"It's good weather for working," Mr. Stafford said, as he swept down cobwebs, removed an old chipmunk nest from inside the roof, and began to chink the spaces between the logs.

"It's also good weather to find out if we really like island life," Mrs. Stafford remarked, bringing in a plate of fresh, buttered bread spread with strawberry preserves. "Almost anyone would love it here when the sun shines, but things are different when it rains."

"We're going to love it in any weather."

John spoke firmly. He was thinking that he would have hated all this cleaning in an ordinary house, but here even scrubbing was exciting. You never knew what you might find when all the dirt and clutter and cobwebs were removed.

He would start to clean a window and then his mind would wander. He'd imagine himself a famous explorer or he'd wonder about the pioneers who had settled these islands and lived in log houses like the small ones behind the mansion. He thought of James Gregor, the prospector, and the other adventurers from all over the world who had come by stagecoach, boat, and even by foot, lured by that magic word — *gold*.

Linda would tug his arm to bring him back to the present and he'd go to work again until the rain let up. Then he'd announce, "It's stopped!" and their father would say, "Okay,

everyone take a break until the next shower."
John and Linda would dash out the door, and
Ricky would appear out of nowhere. (Where
does that kid disappear to? John kept asking
himself.)

Sometimes when the rain stopped they
worked on the garden or went off in the boat,
over to a neighboring island to pick up mail
and supplies. But mostly they used the breaks
between the showers to hurry to the beach.

Ricky liked to run along the sand, pulling
long strings of bladder-wrack and kelp. He
also spent hours making rafts from pieces of
driftwood tied together with old rope.

While their young brother was busy this
way, John and Linda looked for caves where
James Gregor's gold might be hidden. Whenever the tide was out, they wandered into the
shallow water to inspect the cliffs. They found
lots of cracks and crevices. One hole even
looked as though it might be the entrance to
a real cave, but it was too small for them to
squeeze through. John tried, but couldn't get
any farther than his shoulders. When Linda
tried she got stuck, and John had to pull hard
to get her out.

"All I could see was a lot of rocks and some
old driftwood and rope." Linda rubbed her
bruised hips. "What makes you so sure the

gold is in a cave?" she asked. "It could be hidden in a hollow tree or under an old stump or any place."

John looked around to make sure no one was listening. Then he said softly, "You know how detectives try to reconstruct a crime when they want to solve a mystery? Well, that's what I've been doing.

"I've been trying to figure out what James Gregor would have done when he found himself washed up on a rock near this beach. He didn't drown, remember. Captain Sam told us that. He died of exposure because he wasn't found for weeks. So before we can decide what he would have done, we have to think what kind of a man he was."

"He was a mean and suspicious man," Linda replied promptly. "He didn't trust anyone and that's why he set sail on his own."

"Right." John nodded. "So what would a person like that be thinking while he was waiting to be found? He would hope to be rescued, of course, but wouldn't he also be worried about the rescuers stealing his gold? Wouldn't he want to hide it, then come back for it one day? But he couldn't go looking all over the island for a good hiding place. He was wet and cold and probably injured —"

"So he hid it in the nearest place, which is

the cliffs. Maybe he crawled on his hands and knees —"

"Or maybe he just did this." John picked up a large pebble from the water and aimed it as though he were pitching a baseball. With a thud it entered the hole in the cliff, and Linda watched it thoughtfully.

"I wonder if he would have been strong enough to throw it after his accident," she said doubtfully. "Still the tide might have washed it in by itself. If James Gregor was lying on these rocks and the gold was beside him — look, John, that's what I mean."

A large wave was coming toward them, picking up pieces of rope and driftwood that were lying on the beach. The wave hit the rocks and spray flew upward. Water poured into the hole in the cliff, carrying some of the debris along with it.

"There must be all kinds of things in there." John jumped up, peering at the cliff. "Maybe I could attach a big magnet to a piece of old chain and see what it would pick up. Or just keep on poking away at the hole till we make it big enough to squeeze through. Then when we get inside — then we'll find the gold."

John's face was bright, but Linda seemed hesitant. "What about — you know — the *thing*? I can't help thinking about it. What if

76

it comes again? We might not even know it's here —"

"We'll know, Lin, because I'm going to build a lookout, and then we'll be able to keep guard and see anyone or anything heading this way. We can take turns watching."

"That's a great idea! When will it be ready?" Linda asked eagerly.

"I'm going to start building it just as soon as the weather gets better."

It was the end of the week, though, before the weather finally cleared. John woke up one morning and saw a deep blue sky and bright sunshine. Right away he knew that this was the day for building the lookout.

In the morning the whole family worked on the garden. After lunch Mrs. Stafford announced, "The rest of the day is going to be a holiday. Why don't we celebrate the sunshine with a picnic at the beach."

"I think," John said casually, "that I'll make a start on my tree house instead."

Linda sidled up to him and said in a low voice that she would help, but John shook his head. "I'd sure like your help, Lin, but if you come Rick will want to follow, then Mom and Dad will come too. They might start asking questions."

* * *

He was excited to be working on his lookout at last and happy to be on his own. But gradually, as the sun beat fiercely down on him, he began to think how nice it would be to go for a swim. From his perch in the tree he could see his family at the beach, and they seemed to be having lots of fun, while he was working hard.

His father was fishing for a salmon to wrap in seaweed and bake in hot ashes for supper, and his mother was collecting shells. Linda was swimming energetically, and Ricky was running around cracking a long sea onion. His laughter floated up to John. Then Mom, whose voice carried quite clearly in the still air, was telling Ricky how the Indians used the sea onion stems to make fish traps and lines.

"Maybe," John thought, "I should take a rest for a while and go down to the beach with the others."

But he kept on working. Something made him want to finish the platform that day. Wiping his perspiring face, he went back to hammering boards. He was hot and tired by bedtime, but he had the satisfaction of knowing that the lookout was built. When Linda came to see it, her enthusiasm made him feel even better.

"Now we'll be able to keep watch," she said. "Now we'll find out who keeps coming to the island — and why!"

"I hope you're right," said John as they walked back to the floathouse. He felt really happy as he settled wearily into his bunk.

When he awoke next morning he couldn't wait to go and see his lookout again. Even before breakfast he was outside, running through the woods and across the field he called his "ball park." The startled inhabitants greeted him with a great chattering and squawking, although a kingfisher sitting near the river just stared in white-collared dignity.

This morning John ignored them all as he raced up the hill to the craggy plateau and the solitary tree where he had built his platform.

Atop the plateau he stopped dead in his tracks and blinked his eyes. *There was no tree and no platform.* Someone had come in the night and cut it down — someone who intended to make sure that there was no lookout on the island.

The Last Straw

The forlorn looking stump seemed to dance in front of John's eyes. The arbutus tree was lying on the ground. All that was left of the lookout were pieces of lumber scattered among the rocks. Even as he stared at the wreckage, John could hardly believe it was true. The tree had given such a good view. He'd worked so hard to build the lookout. Now they were both gone, never to be replaced. A tree like that took years to grow; and even if he put up a big pole and built another platform, it would probably be chopped down the next day.

Despondently John slumped beside the stump of the tree. It was a shivery feeling to know that someone — or something — was watching everything he did, ready to move against him at any time. And now there was no proper lookout where he could watch for the intruders.

He turned around dejectedly when he heard Linda running up the hill. "Mom says if you want breakfast —" she began.

Then she stopped and stared in disbelief, just as John had done a few minutes earlier. "It's gone! The lookout and everything." She gazed at the stump with shocked eyes. "Oh, John, after all your work. Do you think it was — the *thing*?"

"It was something that could use an axe. Something that didn't even bother to hide the evidence. Probably left it all lying around on purpose, to show us that they'll beat us every time. And maybe they're right. Maybe we haven't got a chance against them."

Head bent, he walked slowly back to the floathouse. He tried to put on a smile for his mother so she wouldn't know that anything was wrong, but it wasn't a very convincing smile.

Mrs. Stafford started to scold, then broke off when she saw his face. Quietly she placed his food in front of him and didn't ask any questions, for which John was thankful. He didn't feel like talking just now. In fact, for the first time since he could remember, he didn't even feel like eating. John, who always finished the rest of the family's leftovers, now pushed his plate away almost untouched.

It wasn't just the loss of the lookout. It was a general feeling of failure. After a whole week of hammering at the cliff, he still hadn't made the hole any bigger. He hadn't even found Ricky's hiding place and that annoyed him, though he was sure his brother's secret wasn't anything of importance.

Helping his father build new kitchen cupboards, John was very quiet and depressed. If he didn't solve the mystery soon, they might never live in this house. They might have to leave the island. That was such an awful thought it brought a tight lump into his throat, and when his father tried to start a conversation, he couldn't answer.

At ten o'clock Mrs. Stafford came in from working in the garden. She looked at John, then talked to her husband in a low voice for several minutes. Mr. Stafford listened and nodded.

"Captain Sam taught you and Linda to handle the boat, didn't he, John?"

"Sure." John looked up, startled out of his gloom.

"Well, how would you two like to take her out today? Mom and I have a lot to do, and we thought perhaps you could go for the mail and groceries."

"You mean — just Lin and me? No one else?" So far they had always gone out in the boat as a family, with Mr. Stafford in charge.

His father nodded. "Just you and Lin. But don't let Rick know you're going, or he'll want to go too."

Mrs. Stafford said, "I've written out a list of groceries we need, but you don't have to rush straight back. If you meet any young people, you can stay for a while."

So that was it. A smile of understanding spread over John's face. Mom thought his unhappiness this morning was due to lack of friends. That was why she had cooked up this idea. Well, it was better than having her suspect the real reason, and it gave him a chance to use the boat. Nothing could have been more effective in banishing his depression.

"When can we start?" he asked eagerly.

"Right now. Lin's at the dock with the grocery list."

John didn't waste another minute. He rushed out the door, dashing through the tangle of long grass and weeds they would cut as soon as the scythe arrived from Victoria. He was in such a hurry that he didn't see the hole until his foot slipped down inside it, throwing him to the ground. And it was then, while he was lying on his chest, that he saw the small wooden door.

Excitedly he wriggled forward on his stomach, reaching his hand out to the door and slowly beginning to open it. Suddenly the door was wrenched out of his hand and a furious little figure burst through.

"This is my place. You keep away. It's mine!"

"Ricky!" John sat up in surprise. So this was the secret hiding place. He saw that the door was built into a knoll or rise in the land and hidden by the tall grass.

"You keep away from here," Rick stormed, and Mrs. Stafford, hearing his raised voice, came hurrying toward them.

"What's all the commotion? What's going on? Ricky, you'll get spanked if you talk so rudely."

She looked at the angry little boy, and at John sitting in the tall grass. Then she bent down and saw the door.

"A root cellar," she exclaimed delightedly. "That's where Lee Jang must have stored his root vegetables in the winter. And that hole is where he kept his milk and butter and cheese. He probably put wire netting over the top to keep the animals away, and since it never gets too cold in these parts, the food would have kept cool and fresh without freezing."

"Sort of a primitive refrigerator," John said. But just now he was more interested in the inside of the root cellar, since his foot had told him there was nothing inside the hole. He pushed open the door, snapping on the flashlight he always carried in his pocket. It certainly seemed empty, but he decided to investigate more fully later on. He wasn't going to let Rick have it all to himself.

A few minutes later John and Linda were skimming over the water — just the two of them, with no adults to tell them what to do. The water was clear and calm and the boat handled beautifully. They soon reached their destination and tied up at the wharf, where they saw a group of kids carrying baseball bats and mitts.

"Going to have a game?" John asked. "Have you got a good field here?"

"Pretty good," one of the boys answered. "Would you like to play? We could use a couple more kids."

Would he like to play! In the first ten minutes John managed a home run, and Linda distinguished herself with a spectacular catch.

They played for almost an hour and enjoyed every minute.

Happy and hot after the game, most of the players gathered at the store, where they drank soda and ate ice cream cones. They introduced themselves: Pete and Nancy Stevens on vacation from Oregon, the Benson twins from Alberta, and two local kids, Stell Perkins and Dave Lowe. They were friendly and good fun, and they all agreed to get together again soon.

"How about coming to our place?" John said. "We're just up the channel." He pointed. "You can't see it because it's around the point, but it's just a short boat ride."

He heard a gasp and found Stell and Dave regarding him with wide eyes. "You live there?" Dave's voice was incredulous. "You live on Disaster Island?"

Linda said hotly, "Don't use that stupid name. It's Stafford Island now and it's a great place."

"I wouldn't be you." Stell drew back as though afraid of catching something. "Everyone knows Disaster Island's haunted. Only bad things happen there."

"What kinds of things?" John tried to keep his voice bright, but he had a sinking feeling inside. That name again. That drawing back. "Have you ever been there?" he asked.

"I sure haven't, and I wouldn't go. No one goes over there."

"And even if we wanted to, our folks wouldn't let us." Dave gave the clincher before turning and walking away.

John spoke quickly to the other kids. "You're not going to be scared off by silly rumors, are you? How about coming and seeing for yourselves — then you can tell those guys!"

"We've got to get permission before we can go off any place." Pete Stevens didn't meet his eyes. A few minutes ago he had been so friendly, and now everything had changed. "We'll ask our parents and next time you come over we'll tell you. Okay?"

"Okay." But John knew what the answer would be. He felt cold inside as he picked up the mail and packed the groceries into the boat.

"Suppose everyone feels the same way?" Linda spoke suddenly as they set course for home. "Suppose no one wants to come to our island even when we've got it all fixed up and ready?"

John swallowed hard. This was the thing

that worried him the most. If no visitors came
they'd have to give up the island. They'd have
used up all their money by then, they'd have
no place to live, and it would be mostly his
fault because he was the one who had pushed
and persuaded his parents to buy the island.

He had to do something about it — but
what? How could he stop those awful rumors?
How could he persuade people to come and see
for themselves? He couldn't think of any way,
and Linda couldn't either. They were still trying to figure out what to do when they tied up
at their own dock and saw a familiar figure
waiting for them.

"Captain Sam!" They threw themselves on
him. "Why didn't you tell us you were coming?
We wouldn't have gone away!"

"It was quite unexpected." The captain
hugged them both. "I called your father on
the radio phone, but you had already left. Anyway, this is just a short visit." He leaned forward. "I've brought you your first visitors —
Mr. and Mrs. Telford."

Smiling, he pointed to the path where Mr.
and Mrs. Stafford were talking to a young
couple.

"They're just married," the captain went
on, "and they're at the university. I met them
in the library this morning and they happened

to mention that they were looking for a place for the summer that would be inexpensive and quiet enough for them to study. So I brought them here right away."

"And do they like it?" John hardly dared to ask, but the captain nodded vigorously.

"Sure do. Just what they want, they said. I'm bringing them back next week to stay the rest of the summer. Your dad said he could have one of the cabins ready by then."

"Oh boy!" John and Linda looked at each other delightedly. Their first visitors — and long before they had expected. How silly they had been to think no one would want to come here. Sensible people wouldn't be scared off by stupid rumors.

John would have liked to talk to Captain Sam and tell him about the peculiar things that had been happening. But the Telfords had to be taken back to Victoria and there was no time for talking.

"I'll be back soon," the captain said cheerfully, and that was something to look forward to. In fact, everything seemed fine now that the first visitors were coming. With so much work to do there was no time for worrying anyway.

They chose the cabin that was in the best condition, then cleaned it inside and out. The roof had to be fixed where it leaked, new glass put in the windows that were broken, new wiring installed, and the sagging steps made secure.

Everyone pitched in to help, and no one minded the work because they were so pleased to be having their first visitors. Even the small amount of money the Telfords would pay would be a help. But most important, they would go back to Victoria and tell people how nice the island was. Then next summer, when everything was ready, there would be lots of vacationers wanting to come and visit.

"Everything is working out very well," John's mother said on Friday, as they sat down to dinner.

"And keeping the kids working hard is a good thing," his father replied. "They're too busy to fight." Then the three of them started to poke at each other, just to show they had enough energy left for that.

It was then, as they were all laughing and feeling good, that the call came through from Captain Sam. The Telfords had changed their minds about coming to the island. "I'll try to find out the reason," the captain said, but John and Linda looked at each other and felt suddenly cold. They knew what the reason would be.

The rumors. Someone had got to the Telfords with stories about the island. Someone had scared them away, as they planned to scare everyone away so that the Stafford family would finally leave the island too.

"We won't go without a fight," John vowed. Inside him a great anger was mounting. This cancelation was the last straw, and now the time had come to fight back.

◆

The Night of the Storm

It was twenty minutes after midnight and the floathouse was quiet. Lying in his bunk, wide awake, John listened to the even breathing coming from the other bunks. Everyone was asleep. Now was the time.

He reached under the sheets for the jeans and sweatshirt he had hidden there. He pulled them over his pajamas, moving carefully so the bed wouldn't creak and wake anyone. He tiptoed across the floor, opened the door, and silently closed it behind him. He'd done it! He was out, and no one knew he had gone. The first part of his plan was accomplished.

He had his flashlight, but he didn't need it. The night was clear, with a fresh wind dispersing the clouds and a bright moon lighting up the sky.

"Perfect," John told himself. "Visibility will be one hundred percent."

But he shivered a little as he looked around. Everything seemed so different when you were outdoors alone at night. Behind him the water, churned up by the wind, was dashing white-caps against the shore. In front the tall trees bent and creaked, looking strange and shadowy.

John felt a funny little tingle in the bottom of his stomach. When he had made his plans he'd been so busy working out what to do he hadn't thought of the scary part. Now he felt a sudden urge to bolt back into the safety of the floathouse.

But he knew that this was something he had to do. It wasn't fun and it wasn't playacting. This was real and serious. He drew a deep breath and started slowly along the path.

In the leaves beneath his feet there was a rustling sound as moles and shrews moved about. In the air there was the whirring and buzzing of summer bugs. Several times he turned on his flashlight to investigate some unusual sound. A few times he drew back with a gasp as a shadow moved menacingly toward him. But each time it turned out to be the wind whistling through a hollow tree, or the sway-

93

ing of an overhanging branch, and John would give a sigh of relief.

It seemed ages before he reached the end of the path, but finally the old mansion loomed in front of him. It gleamed palely, with a strange, forbidding air. A pair of bats circled wraithlike in front of the entrance as if warning John away.

But he had to go in. That was part of his plan. He had to go inside and up the stairs and out onto the balcony. Slowly he mounted the great steps. He pushed open the heavy door, then jumped, with his hand to his mouth, as the wind banged the door shut behind him.

He felt very small and defenseless in the huge banquet hall. The thin beam from his flashlight didn't chase away the shadows, and the moon's rays hardly penetrated the dirt streaked windows. Cobwebs hung everywhere. In the semidarkness he saw a mouse scuttle into a corner and a bumpy toad hop slowly across the floor.

John gulped. He couldn't help thinking about the ghost that was supposed to have been seen on this island. He couldn't help remembering the rumors that so many people believed.

He wanted to turn and run, but he went on. His footsteps penetrated the silence: *thump,*

thump, thump, like the heavy beating of his heart.

He walked up the stairs holding on to the banister. What if his flashlight petered out? What if he was left here in the darkness, shut in with — who knew what?

But on he went, through a shadowy bedroom to the balcony. Out in the open air it didn't feel so creepy. The moon bathed the island in silvery light. This was what he had come for, the reason he had crept into this haunted looking place all alone. Now that the lookout was gone, there was nowhere else to watch for the intruders, and he had to outwit them somehow.

He looked around for several minutes. The island seemed deserted. There was no sign of movement anywhere — not at the dock, not in the woods, not on the high crag or on the beach. John felt a surge of relief. He had come and seen for himself that everything was quiet, and now he could hurry back to his snug bed. Another night he would come and look again.

But just as he turned to leave, he caught the flicker of a light, a pinprick at first but getting bigger as it came closer and closer to the beach. His ears caught the hum of a motor, and he knew that they had come —

the intruders, the rumor spreaders, the tree choppers.

John stood tensely on the balcony, holding on to the rail. For the first time he wondered if it had been wise to keep the strange happenings from his parents. Maybe he ought to have told his father. Maybe it was too big for him and Linda to handle on their own.

But there was no time to worry about that now. If he wanted to find out what was going on, he would have to head for the beach at once. Quickly, before he lost his nerve, he hurried down the stairs and out the door. He started out through the woods on the winding trail that led to the beach.

But the wind had grown much stronger. It beat at him with heavy gusts, trying to push him down. It shook the trees until they shivered and moaned, their leaves whirling dizzily around his head.

Half blinded by flying debris, deafened by the howling wind, John groped his way along. He stumbled on an unseen rock. He slipped on a moss-covered log. A falling branch caught him, tearing a hole in his pants and making a long, jagged scratch on his leg. And while he was wiping away the blood, the wind knocked him down.

Once more he struggled to his feet. Through

the wildly shaking trees he could still see the glimmering light on the beach, and he knew he had to go on.

With each gust of wind John wondered about the floathouse. Was it safe and still anchored at the wharf? Had his parents been awakened by the noise? Had they discovered that he was missing?

"Just a little farther," he kept telling himself. "Just a little farther. I'm almost there."

His leg was hurting where the branch had hit it. His eyes were sore and his back ached from battling the force of the wind. But slowly, bit by bit, he moved forward until at last he was on the bluff above the beach.

He could see two shadowy figures moving around on the beach. But when he leaned forward to see more clearly, the wind immediately tried to blow him down — straight down the path to the beach, into the hands of the enemy.

Quickly he grabbed the trunk of a spruce tree. Then he lay flat on his stomach and peered downward.

Suddenly he heard an ominous creak. A great gust of wind blew above his head and the tree beside him began to tilt. John scrambled to his feet. With one great bound he jumped out of the way, just as the tree crashed to the ground on the very spot where he had been lying.

John could hardly breathe. He stared at the tree in horror. Another minute, another fraction — if it had fallen on him, he would have been crushed beneath its weight. He shuddered and closed his eyes.

When he opened them again, the light on the beach and the two shadowy figures were gone. John could hear the throb of a motor as the boat began to move. Then the sound faded and he couldn't hear anything but the wind.

Without stopping to think of danger, he sat down on the ground and slid, on the seat of his pants, down the sandy path to the beach. There had to be some clue to show him who had been here and why. After all he had gone through tonight, he couldn't go back with no more evidence than before.

The waves were beating against the shore, soaking him with a torrent of spray, but John didn't care. Slowly he walked along the shore, searching intently for some sign. And then he saw it and drew back with a gasp, while a shiver of fear ran through him.

On the wet sand was the clear imprint of a foot — a footmark that looked neither human nor animal. It looked like the track of a giant with webbed feet!

Down, Down, Down

John looked around to make sure no one could overhear. Then he turned to Linda. "Now that we're alone," he said softly, "I've got lots of things to tell you."

This was the first chance he'd had since last night to talk to Linda privately. Since early morning the whole family had been working on Operation Clean-Up — clearing the paths of branches that had fallen during the storm.

Now it was seven o'clock and they were all relaxing on the beach after a picnic supper. It was beautifully calm, very different from last night's turbulence. Mr. and Mrs. Stafford were reading the newspaper. Ricky was collecting pieces of driftwood to make a raft. Farther down the beach John and Linda were hacking at the cave opening in the cliffs.

"I knew you'd been up to something last night." Linda looked at her brother with a grin. "Maybe you could fool Mom and Dad with the story that you'd just gone out to see what was happening —"

"It was true," John said defensively. "I did go out to see what was happening. I didn't tell them all the details, that's all."

Then in a low voice he proceeded to tell Linda the whole story, leaving nothing out from the time he made the plan until he saw the webbed footprint in the sand.

Linda listened, her eyes growing bigger and bigger. When John described how he had walked through the spooky mansion, she shivered. When he came to the part where the tree had almost fallen on him, she gasped out loud. At the end, she looked at him with concern.

"You could have been killed. *Anything* could have happened to you. Weren't you scared?"

John touched the long, jagged scratch on his leg. "Sure I was scared, but there won't be a storm every time I keep watch. Anyway, they say the first time is always the worst."

"You mean you're going again? All by yourself in the middle of the night? What if something goes wrong?"

John looked at his sister soberly. "Something is going to go very wrong if we don't solve this mystery. We're going to lose the island. These people are trying to drive us away. I know they are. They chopped down my lookout. They cut the chains of our dock. And they're spreading rumors so no one wants to come here. You remember what Dad said about spending our savings on fixing up this place? If we don't get some people coming here to stay, we won't have any money to keep up the payments and we'll lose everything."

"Yes, I know." Linda's voice was worried.

"So that's why I have to keep watch till I find out what's going on. Why do these people come to our beach in the dark? Who are they, and what do they want? If I hadn't promised Captain Sam not to take the boat out around here, maybe I could find some clues —"

"John, you won't! It's dangerous, and you promised —"

"Don't panic. I won't do it. But I am going to the balcony every night I can get out, and if there are lights on the beach, I'm going to investigate."

"You can't do it by yourself. There are two of them and one is — I don't know *what*." She drew a deep breath. "If you're going to investigate, I'm going to help." Though her voice quivered, her eyes were steady. She wasn't going to let her brother face all the risks alone.

"Good." John grasped her hand. "I've been thinking this out and I do need your help. I don't want you to come with me because, for one thing, I don't think we could both get out without being heard. Another thing — well, if we run into any trouble it's no use both of us being caught, with no one to go for help. So what I'd like you to do is to stay awake on the nights I go out, and if I'm not back in about two hours you can wake Dad and tell him. What do you think of that idea?"

"It's okay, John, and I'll do it of course, but —" Linda was silent for a moment, her head bent. "I know we decided to solve this mystery ourselves without worrying Mom and Dad, but don't you think maybe it's getting too big for us to handle? Maybe they ought to know what's going on."

"I was thinking the same thing last night."

"You were?" Linda had been feeling embarrassed. Now she looked relieved at John's answer.

"Then this morning," John went on, "while we were carting the trees away, I heard Dad say that he had to see the doctor for a checkup."

"So we can't tell him anything that might worry him until after we hear what the doctor says?"

John nodded. "Both he and Mom are going to the mainland on Wednesday, and they'll be away for a couple of days. Captain Sam is coming to stay with us while they're gone."

"Captain Sam!" Linda's voice rose in such a delighted squeal that John looked around to see if anyone had heard. "That's the answer," she said excitedly. "Don't you see? We can tell Captain Sam everything, and he'll know the best thing to do. He's on our side, John. He knows about this kind of thing, and he's the best person in the world to help us. It's only a few days till Wednesday. We can wait till then, can't we?"

"I guess we can." John considered the idea. It *was* a bit scary to take the whole responsibility, and as Linda had said, the captain would be sure to give them good advice. He wouldn't treat them like babies either and say this was something just for adults to deal with.

"All right," he said finally, "I'll wait and speak to Captain Sam before doing anything."

Mr. and Mrs. Stafford left Wednesday morning at ten o'clock. Captain Sam was supposed to arrive about noon. Ricky set out his

103

shell collection on the bunks. In the tiny kitchen, while he and Linda made three-decker sandwiches for lunch, John went over all the details of the story he had to tell.

At one o'clock a message came from the captain over the radio telephone. Something had gone wrong with the engine on his boat and it was taking quite a long time to fix. But they shouldn't worry. He'd be late, but he'd get there for sure.

Hours went by. They ate the sandwiches, then at five o'clock they had the supper Mom had left. They cleaned up the floathouse and waited again, scanning the water for any sign of a boat. No one wanted to leave the dock in case Captain Sam arrived while they were gone. They couldn't go out looking for him because their parents had taken the boat.

Time passed very slowly. It was after nine and getting dark when Captain Sam finally came in sight. Ricky was already asleep. John and Linda ran to the dock but stopped in their eager greetings when they saw how rumpled, tired, and cross their friend looked.

"Very queer, very queer," the captain was mumbling. "I swear someone must have tampered with the engine. All kinds of parts were missing. I had the devil's own job fixing it up

104

again. Never known such a thing to happen before. Can't understand it at all."

John and Linda looked at one another. They understood all right. It all fitted in. Another link in the chain of evidence. Someone had intercepted Mr. Stafford's call to Captain Sam, then tampered with the captain's boat to try to prevent his coming to the island today.

"All kinds of strange things are going on," John began. The story was practically bursting out of him, but before he could say any more, the captain gave a huge yawn.

"I don't know about you youngsters," he said, "but I've had a tough day and I'm beat. It's straight to bed for me."

His blue eyes, usually so bright, were clouded with fatigue. This was no time to tell him a long story or to ask for help and advice.

"Tomorrow," the captain said, "we'll talk." But as far as John was concerned, tomorrow was too late. If *they* had taken the captain's engine apart, hoping to stop him from getting to the island today, it probably meant they planned to come themselves tonight. And John intended to be right there to see what went on.

He had no difficulty slipping out of the floathouse around midnight, when the others were fast asleep. The night was calm, with a big, bright moon and a sky full of stars.

It was much easier this time to walk along the path, and even the old mansion didn't seem as spooky as before. John strode upstairs without a glance to right or left. Out on the balcony, his eyes went straight to the beach, and in the first glance he saw the light of an approaching boat. Instantly he turned, dashed down the stairs and ran along the trail to the beach. He wanted to watch the boat land, see the occupants come out, and find out what they had come to do.

The night was very quiet, with just the muffled hum of the motor down below and the occasional squawk of a heron overhead.

At the end of the trail, where it turned down to the beach, lay the big spruce tree that had fallen in the storm. It had been too heavy to carry away, and since it was at the top of the cliff, away from the main path, Mr. Stafford had just left it there. Now John decided it would be a good shield to crouch behind while he watched the water.

He moved toward the fallen tree, treading carefully among the spreading branches. Looking down once, he saw two shadowy figures emerging from the boat. Then his foot touched an unseen branch that snapped with a crack, like a pistol shot shattering the silence of the night.

John froze. His heart was pounding so fast he could hardly breathe. Instinctively he ducked as a hard bright beam lit up the night. A powerful spotlight stabbed through the darkness from the beached boat and swept across the cliff.

Blinded by the light, John became entangled in the branches of the fallen tree. He struggled frantically to free himself. With a great heave he finally broke loose. But the effect was so great that he lost his balance and fell heavily, hitting his head on a rock.

Everything went black. His knees buckled under him, the ground seemed to give way beneath his body, and he was falling, down, down, down. . . .

◆

Trapped!

Slowly John opened his eyes. His lids were almost too heavy to lift and everything looked blurred. He blinked dizzily, not quite sure he was awake. His bed felt very hard and there was something sharp pressing into his back.

With his fingers he groped beneath his body, pulling out a small, pointed rock. How did that get there? he wondered. His head ached too, and when he put his hand to the pain, he felt a swelling the size of an egg.

Carefully John touched the bump on the back of his head. When had that happened? He couldn't remember hurting his head. There seemed to be all kinds of things he couldn't remember. He was sure this wasn't his bunk he was lying on — and if he wasn't in his own bed, where was he?

His mind felt foggy, and his eyes didn't seem to be focusing properly. Cautiously he groped around with his hands. As far as he could tell he was lying on a hill, with his head and shoulders on soft earth and the rest of his body on small, sharp rocks.

There was a bright patch of moonlight coming from above. If he could get closer to it, maybe he would be able to see where he was. He raised himself into a sitting position and tilted his head to look upward. The bump ached furiously, but he forced himself to look up at the patch of light. As his eyes began to focus, he saw a jagged hole directly above, with part of a tree sticking through.

A hole in the ceiling with a tree in it? What kind of a place was he in? He closed his eyes as though to shut out the vision, but when he opened them again, the hole and the tree were still there.

"I need a light," John muttered. "I can't figure this out." He reached into his pocket where he always kept a flashlight. Holding the light in his hand, he gazed at it intently while something stirred in his memory. The boat ... the beach ...

Memory came rushing back and hurriedly, with the help of a nearby rock, he pulled himself to his feet — only to fall right down again

109

with a gasp of pain. His ankle, his left ankle, wouldn't hold him. He must have injured it when he fell, and now he couldn't stand on it even for a minute.

"I can't be stuck here. I've got to get out." He looked at his foot as though to force it to behave. He tried to stand, slowly and carefully this time, first planting his right foot down firmly — then, very gently, his left.

But it was exactly the same as before. The moment his left foot touched the ground he felt pain shoot through his ankle, and his leg buckled under him. He couldn't even stand, let alone climb the rock that led to the hole above. He was trapped here in this tunnel, while outside something important was going on. And he was powerless to prevent it — or even find out what it was all about.

Probably he wouldn't be found for hours, because no one knew he was missing. When Captain Sam had told him about his engine, he'd been so anxious to start investigating that he'd forgotten to tell Linda he was going out tonight. Now Linda would be fast asleep and she'd stay that way until someone woke her in the morning. The way she could sleep through all kinds of noise was a family joke, like John's bottomless appetite.

But it was no longer a joke to John. It was

terrible to know that the enemy was at the beach while he was stuck, unable to get out.

"Darned ankle." With his good foot he kicked at a piece of driftwood. Suddenly he stopped and stared at it, then cautiously flashed his light around.

Driftwood was brought in by the tide, wasn't it? So how did so much of it get in here? It hadn't come from the break in the earth beneath the tree, because there was no driftwood there. So that meant there was another opening somewhere, one that was near the water, and an old opening too from the look of some of the wood. Maybe it would be easier to get out of than the one up above. Maybe he could escape that way.

With new hope flooding through him, John's mind worked at top speed. People with injured ankles didn't have to sit still all the time. Maybe they couldn't scale a wall of rock, but they could get around with a crutch or a sturdy stick.

He searched through the driftwood until he found a good strong piece the right height. Then, standing on his good foot and leaning heavily on the stick, he managed to hop toward a patch of moonlight he could now see a few yards away.

It wasn't easy and it wasn't fast. His left

111

shoulder ached from the strain and he had to be very careful not to slip. John was panting with exhaustion when he reached the patch of light, but he forgot it all in a cry of triumph when he saw that there was indeed another opening, just as he had figured.

The hole was low and round and near the water, and John could see how driftwood would be tossed in by the tide. Quickly he lowered himself and tried to squeeze through but found that he could get no farther than his shoulders. There was no escape. All his efforts had been for nothing.

At first he was so disappointed he could think of nothing else, but then he realized that his efforts had not been entirely wasted. Though he couldn't get out through the opening, he could see through it, and with the moon so bright he had a good view of the beach.

He could see the outlines of a boat, and a short, heavy-set man standing near it, holding a lantern. The man's lips were moving as though he were speaking to someone, and he was looking out to sea. John followed his gaze, and then his eyes widened and his mouth opened in a silent gasp.

Rising out of the water was a frightening

specter — a tall, black figure with a great head, a humped back, and huge webbed feet. As it walked toward the beach, the light from the lantern shone on it, throwing a shadow on the sand, a shadow of exactly the same shape as John and Linda had seen the night they kept watch outdoors.

John could feel his whole body stiffen. As he watched tensely, the man with the lantern moved closer, and John found himself staring at a diver in a scuba outfit.

The great head was an underwater mask with an air regulator connected to a mouthpiece. The humped back was the compressed air tank, and the webbed feet were rubber flippers.

"Am I ever a landlubber not to have guessed before!" John beat on the rocks with his fists. "I'll never be fooled by a diving suit again, that's for sure."

He stopped muttering abruptly as the diver lifted up his hands and took off his "head." In the light of the lantern, the face was clearly visible — a face that John knew. He had seen it at the motel where they had stayed, before they moved to the island.

"Leonard Greaves!" John whispered the words under his breath. Leonard Greaves, who had tried to turn them against the island from the start. Then John recognized the other man too. It was Harry Abbott, the real estate man Greaves had sent them to see.

From the beginning John had suspected these two, but the enormous footprint and the horrible shadow had put him off the track. Now everything fitted together and at last he understood.

Leonard Greaves and Harry Abbott had wanted the island to themselves because they were searching for James Gregor's gold. They weren't probing the cliffs or digging for it. They were diving for it in the water. Greaves had an underwater light in his hand and he must have used it to search for the long-lost gold at the bottom of the sea. But judging by the disappointed expressions on the men's faces, they had not yet found any gold.

"And they won't find it," John thought fiercely. "They won't find it because it isn't in the water. It's in the cave —"

He broke off suddenly, sucking in his breath. *This was the cave! He was inside it now!*

It was the only part of the cliff that had a hole in it this size. When he reached through, he could even feel the hammer marks where he and Lin had tried to make it bigger. How hard and how often they had worked to get inside, and now here he was. He ought to watch the men outside to see what they were doing, but he just had to start searching right away.

In his excitement, John completely forgot about his injured ankle. Impatiently he stood up on both feet, and immediately went crashing down, knocking driftwood in all directions.

Behind an old piece of wood, dislodged from its place against the wall, John spotted a rusty metal box with two large letters engraved on it. The letters were J. G.

"James Gregor!" John's lips formed the words. It was the gold! He had found it at last, just as he'd imagined it so many times.

He remembered discussing it with Linda on the beach, when he had explained why the gold would be in this cave. He recalled tossing a pebble through the hole to show how James Gregor might have hidden his gold to keep it safe. He had pointed out how the tide came in carrying logs and rope and tossing them into the cave — another reason to believe the gold would be there, Lin had agreed.

But in spite of all his talk he had never been completely certain that he was right. It had only been a theory. Now he knew for sure: he had been right all the time. The gold was here, he was looking at it and all he had to do was to stretch out his hand!

Even as he leaned toward it, though, even as his fingers closed around the box, he heard the sound of running footsteps overhead. Had the men in the boat seen a light in the cave?

♦

Footsteps

With his fingers still clutching the precious box, John froze. The hair on the back of his neck seemed to stand on end, and his ears strained to catch every sound from above.

The footsteps were coming closer . . . they had reached the very spot where the earth had given way . . .

John waited, holding his breath. But strangely, the footsteps had stopped. All was silent overhead. No head appeared to glare down at him. No menacing figure came sliding down the slope.

Maybe the crack in the earth wasn't easy to see. Maybe it was hidden underneath the tree. Several seconds ticked by with no movement or sound and gradually John's tense muscles began to relax. But even though the danger was over for the moment, he felt it was still lurking there, ready to pounce. He had to use this short breathing spell to think of the best thing to do. Leonard Greaves wasn't the type to give up easily, and if he poked around long enough, he'd be sure to find where the ground had given way.

John swallowed. The husky diver was twice his size, and much stronger. With an injured foot and no weapon John couldn't possibly defend himself. Maybe the thing to do was to hide, to crawl into the darkest corner of the cave and make himself small.

He rejected that idea almost immediately. The two men had a lantern, and there was the big spotlight on the boat. Once the cave was lit, there would be no place to hide. They would catch him in a minute and they would see the treasure —

John clutched the box tightly. He had to think of something soon. He could hear footsteps starting up again, moving back and forth. The men were still searching, looking for him. He couldn't hope to escape detection for long.

Suppose he hid the box at the back of the cave, in a safe place where he could find it tomorrow, then lay down on the ground pretending to be unconscious? But anybody who'd ever watched television knew about that trick, and John didn't really think he could fool Leonard Greaves and Harry Abbott that way. He thought about the spear gun he had seen on the beach, the sharp, pointed weapon that divers used for spearing fish under water. One prod with that and he wouldn't be able to keep up the pretense of unconsciousness.

There had to be *some* way. He couldn't just stay here waiting to be discovered. If his foot weren't injured, he'd take the chance of climbing out and making a dash for the floathouse.

He looked down at his ankle. It seemed to be getting more swollen by the minute, and there was a purple bruise on one side. But when he looked down at the bruise, John noticed something that worried him even more — water was lapping around his feet.

He had been so intent on what was happening overhead that he hadn't noticed the change inside the cave. Now a feeling of terror came over him. With each wave that pounded against the cliff, the water spreading over the floor of the cave grew a little deeper.

The tide was coming in, and when the tide came in, John knew, water poured into the hole. He had seen it that way lots of times when he was swimming. He and Linda had been able to work on the hole only at low tide.

How far would the water come into the cave? It would come to the top of the hole for certain, and that was well above John's knees. Would it eventually rise above his head? He couldn't see any water mark on the walls; but when he pulled himself up and stretched out his hand to the rocky wall, it was damp to the touch at shoulder height.

John's stomach lurched at this new and dangerous threat. As he watched the water rising higher, he knew there was no time to lose. *He had to get out of the cave.* He had to climb out the way he had fallen in.

With every sense sharpened by the danger, he examined first the wall of rock, then the soft earth above it, and finally the jagged crack with the branch of the fallen tree sticking through. If he could reach the earthy patch, he might be able to manage. But how could he get there? There wasn't even a toe-hold on the smooth sheet of rock he had to scale in order to reach the layer of earth.

Driftwood was no use in a situation like this. Small pieces of rock wouldn't help. He didn't know what would help until he remembered seeing a piece of rope in a corner. Then a plan flashed into his mind.

The rope was old and damp, but it wasn't frayed anywhere and it was long enough for his purpose. Would it also be strong enough? That was something he didn't dare think about right now.

The rising water was already creeping up his legs. The dampness of the wall penetrated his sleeve as he leaned against it for support. With the knowledge of danger both above and below, John worked feverishly to tie a loop in the rope. The long hours he had spent practicing knots for Scout badges were paying off.

Now he sat on the floor, directly beneath the crack that he had fallen through, trying to throw the loop around the protruding branch. Again and again he tried, and each time he missed. If he could stand up to throw, it would be easier — but then he would only be able to use one hand, because the other would have to hold the stick to support his injured foot.

Carefully he moved into a kneeling position. His hands shook with urgency as the sound of beating waves grew louder at his back.

With all his strength he once more flung the rope at the tree. He held his breath, then let it out in a sharp gasp of relief, for this time, at last, the loop had gone over the branch. Quickly he pulled the rope taut; then, holding on tightly with both hands, he swung himself up from the ground.

121

He had already decided to take James Gregor's box with him. He couldn't bear to leave it behind. But since he needed both hands free, he tucked the box inside his roomy sweatshirt, tucked the sweatshirt inside his jeans, and tightened his belt.

Grimly he began to shinny up the rope, using his knees and trying not to bump his injured ankle. The branch quivered under his weight, and the old rope jerked as he pulled on it. "Let it hold," John whispered fiercely. "Please, let it hold."

As he slowly pulled himself up, the rough cord bit into his hands. His shoulders felt as though they couldn't bear the load another minute, and his knees ached terribly.

He was nearing the top. He hardly dared glance at the heaving branch, which bent a little further with each tug of the rope. If it gave way now, he'd go crashing all the way down.

"No!" John shook his head to push the thought away. Right now, he just had to keep on climbing, looking neither up nor down.

Finally he pulled himself up the last stretch of rope. Then, bracing himself, he grabbed for the swaying branch. It broke with a snap beneath his hands and the rope went spilling back down into the depths of the cave. But even as the branch broke, John rolled onto the ledge of soft earth. He lay there panting, eyes closed, while the tension flowed out of his body like air from a torn balloon.

He'd made it. He was out of the cave. One danger had been beaten. But what about the other? Had Leonard Greaves heard the snap of the branch? Would it bring him running this way?

With his breath still coming in gasps, John crouched beneath the fallen tree, listening. No one appeared and there was no sound of movement, but John knew that he had to stay alert, prepared to spring into action at the slightest sign of trouble. In the meantime, he had to decide on his next move.

Should he spend the rest of the night here, hoping to escape detection and waiting for Captain Sam and Linda to find him in the morning? Or should he try to make a getaway?

Everything inside him said yes to the second idea. At the floathouse his comfortable bed would be waiting, and there would be food in the refrigerator and Captain Sam to apply first aid to his foot. But getting there would be full of danger. Once he climbed out into the open there would be no place to hide and he couldn't move fast with his injured ankle.

What should he do? For several minutes

John pondered the alternatives, and it wasn't the thought of his bed or the chocolate cake that made him decide to try for the floathouse. It was the box under his sweatshirt.

He drew it out and looked at it, weighing it in his hand and trying to figure how much gold it contained. It was so rusty and tightly sealed that he would need a hacksaw to get it open. And how could he wait all the hours till morning to open it?

John could imagine Linda's eyes getting big when he showed her the box. He could almost hear Captain Sam saying, "You're sure a great detective, John." He could hardly wait to call his father on the radio phone and tell him that their worries about the island were over. What did it matter if it was the middle of the night? News of this kind couldn't wait, and his parents would be thrilled. Just thinking how happy they would be made John want to hurry. Everything was quiet up above, so now was the time to start.

He tucked the box back inside his sweatshirt. Then, leaning against the broken-off branch, he swung his good leg over the trunk of the tree and stood on it firmly. Finally, wincing with pain, he dragged his other leg across.

There was no one in sight, but John was

taking no chances. Silently he crept forward. The fallen tree had dozens of branches, large and small, ready to entangle anyone who didn't take care, ready to snap at the slightest pressure. John figured out each step before he moved, and he was almost in the clear, almost out of reach of the sprawling tree, when a sharp branch caught his belt and held him fast.

Desperately he twisted and squirmed, struggling to pull himself free, and at last managed to disentangle himself. But in the struggle his sweatshirt was pulled out of his jeans and James Gregor's box, the precious box, fell to the ground with a bang and rolled down the path.

Suddenly there came the sound of running footsteps. John made a dive for the box, but as he hit the ground, a sickening pain shot through his leg. For the second time that night he felt himself dissolve into blackness.

◆

The Old Metal Box

When John opened his eyes, he found himself in his own bed in the floathouse. Linda was arranging a pillow underneath his head and Captain Sam was applying an ice pack to his ankle.

John blinked from one to the other. How had he arrived here? What had happened after he fell? And most important of all — where was the box?

The box! He sat up quickly, all else forgotten. Then he saw it on the bed beside him and grabbed it with a smile of relief.

"John, you're all right!" Linda flung her arms around him tightly. "Look, Captain Sam, he's sitting up and he's smiling. Oh, John, we've been so worried. Are you okay?"

"I'm fine."

Holding the precious box, John smiled broadly. He still didn't know what had happened nor how he had got to the floathouse, but he had the gold and he was safe. All he needed now was something to eat. . . .

Linda seemed to read his thoughts. "If you're feeling fine, I bet you're hungry," she said, and she went into the kitchen and brought back a huge slice of cake with ice cream on top. John immediately set to work, and with his mouth full of chocolate icing he asked, "How did I get here? The last thing I remember is making a dive for the box when it fell out of my shirt."

"That was when we found you." Linda sat down on the edge of the bed. "We heard the bang when the box hit the ground, and we came running. Captain Sam made a stretcher from the fallen tree and we carried you here. We've only been back a few minutes."

"But how did you know where I was? You couldn't have heard the noise all the way from here. How did you happen to be out there in the middle of the night?"

"We were looking for you. Don't you remember you said if you weren't back in two hours we should come after you?"

"Yes, but—"

"You thought I didn't know you were going

out tonight." Linda's smile was full of mischief. "You thought I would sleep right through, didn't you? But I guessed you were going and set my alarm for half past twelve, then put it under my pillow so it wouldn't waken anyone else when it rang."

"And when you woke up, you found I was gone."

Linda nodded. "I got dressed and went to sit outside. I was afraid I'd fall asleep again if I waited in bed. But the sound of the waves began to make me sleepy, so I decided to go to the mansion and look out from the balcony —"

"You went there all by yourself at night? Wow, you've sure got a lot of guts."

John's voice was full of admiration and Linda flushed with pleasure. "I won't pretend I wasn't scared," she said. "To tell the truth, I was petrified. But when I got out onto the balcony and saw the light on the beach, I was so excited I guess I forgot to be afraid. I even started out on the path to the beach, but then I remembered what you said about it not doing any good if we both got caught, so I went back and waited."

She grinned. "I didn't wait the full two hours. I just couldn't stand it that long. I woke

Captain Sam and told him everything right from the beginning —"

"And made my hair stand up on end." The captain spoke for the first time. "If anything had happened to you, John boy, I would never have forgiven myself. I knew you wanted to tell me something last night, but I thought it could wait. I was so tired . . ." He passed his hand across his eyes and said sadly, "I'm not as young as I used to be."

"You're in fine shape and so am I, so don't worry." John took a big bite of chocolate cake to show how well he felt. "Everything turned out all right in the end. In fact," he said, running his hand across the rusty metal box, "it was better that I didn't talk to you last night."

If he had confided in the captain, he would not have been able to investigate by himself. Then he never would have fallen into the cave and discovered the gold.

"Of course, it's a good thing you found me when you did. If you hadn't been out looking for me —" He shuddered at the thought that Leonard Greaves or Harry Abbott might have found him and seen James Gregor's box.

"But where were you?" Linda asked. "I looked and looked, but I couldn't find you. Captain Sam went down to the beach to search there. He told those two men he'd tar and feather them if they didn't produce you."

John laughed. That sounded just like the peppery captain. "For a while I didn't even know where I was."

He told the whole story then, from the time he saw the light on the beach until he climbed out of the cave with the box. He spoke slowly, emphasizing each dramatic incident, enjoying the rapt attention he was receiving.

"Now let's open the box," he finished. "We can talk more afterward, but I can't wait another minute to see the gold."

He wanted to know if it was fine placer dust from the sand bars of the Fraser, or nuggets from the Barkerville area. He was anxious to see how much there was.

"We'll need a hacksaw to open the box," he said, as he started to get out of bed. Linda quickly pushed him back.

"I'll get it," she said. "You've got to rest your foot."

She ran to her father's worktable and brought the tool chest. John watched breathlessly as Captain Sam carefully began to cut off the rusty lock. It seemed to him that he had never seen anyone work so slowly. He would have liked to grab the saw from the captain's hand and do the job himself.

After all, it wasn't every day that he found a box of gold, especially famous gold from the Cariboo, mined by those early prospectors who climbed mountain passes and forded rivers —

"There! It's open." Captain Sam held out the box, and John almost dropped it in his eagerness to look inside. As he lunged to catch it, the box opened wide and its contents spilled out on the bed.

Linda gasped and John's eyes popped.

"A book!" John stared at the leather-bound volume as though he'd never seen one before. "A book," he repeated blankly. For a moment he was too stunned to move.

Then he picked up the box and turned it upside down. But nothing fell out. It was quite empty now, and John threw it on the floor and grabbed the book, shaking it violently as though to force something to drop out, some gold dust perhaps, or a nugget or two. There had to be something else besides this old book with its spidery writing and its yellowed pages.

Furious with disappointment, he shook it again and again, until Captain Sam caught his arm and took the book away.

"Stop it, John! Stop it at once! That's James Gregor's diary you've found, and it has to be

131

treated with care. It's a very important document."

His voice softened. "I know you're disappointed. You were expecting gold and you found a book instead. But don't you see you've discovered something that's more important than gold? These old diaries that the pioneers kept are a true record of what really happened. They tell exciting, adventurous stories. And this diary" — he was turning the pages as he spoke — "Oh, this is one of the best! Just wait till they see this in Victoria.

"James Gregor met all the well-known people of his time — like F. J. Barnard, the man who traveled three hundred eighty miles by foot to deliver mail to the gold fields. His name is in here . . . and here's a story about Captain Irvine, the famous riverboat pilot . . . and listen to this, John, Gregor witnessed the stagecoach robbery at Cache Creek! Maybe that's what made him so suspicious of everyone."

The captain's eyes shone and his voice shook with excitement. He would have gone on and on if John hadn't interrupted. "What does he say about the gold he had with him when he was shipwrecked?"

John could feel disappointment like a hard lump inside him, but a ray of hope was breaking through. He had found a diary instead of gold, but the diary might give a clue as to where the gold would be.

"Turn to the back," he said. "Read the end part. Surely he must say something about the gold."

"Yes, yes, I expect there will be something." The captain turned to the back of the diary as John had asked and read silently to himself for a moment. "Yes," he said, "he tells about the gold."

Then, without another word, he handed the book to John.

What Next?

Breathlessly John began to read aloud from James Gregor's diary.

March 15, 1863

I have arrived safely in New Westminster with the gold, but now I find that the steamer to Victoria has been delayed and no one knows when it will arrive.

I am afraid for my gold among this crowd. I have many enemies who would steal the gold from me, and I do not like standing here at the dock, with people pressing all around. Twice already I have been robbed, and I must not lose my last poke of gold, after all my hard labors.

I have decided not to wait for the steamer. It might take all night, I am told. I will get myself a small vessel and

*make the crossing alone. Surely I, who
have traveled the Fraser and the Thomp-
son rivers, can manage the Strait of
Georgia. At least, when I travel alone, I
know that I cannot be robbed.*

With his heart beating fast, John turned
the page. The last paragraphs were written
in a nearly illegible scrawl, and the paper was
stained. John read slowly, struggling to de-
cipher the words.

*I thought I could not be robbed if I
traveled alone, but I forgot that the sea
can be a robber too.*

*The sea has stolen my gold. A fierce
squall overturned my small craft, and the
wind snatched and ripped open my carefully tied poke. Though I dived through
the water after it, the wind beating
against me was too strong. Before my
very eyes, the gold scattered on the waves
and sank to the bottom of the sea.*

*Now I drift helplessly in the leaking
boat. Only God knows where I will land
or what will happen to me. This diary in
its tin box is all that I managed to save.
I have no food, no dry clothes; I burn with
fever. And all for the gold, the rich yellow
dust that is gone and lost for ever.*

John's voice stopped, but in the quiet of the

floathouse his words still hung in the air: *All for the gold, the rich yellow dust that is gone and lost for ever.*

"Leonard Greaves figured it out better than I did," John blurted out bitterly. "At least he was on the right track when he went diving for the gold. Maybe he'll even find it someday!"

"No, John." Captain Sam picked up the diary. "Greaves and Abbott were looking for the remains of the boat in the water. They probably hoped to find a leather poke full of nuggets. But when you read this diary you'll see that James Gregor was carrying flour, which is very fine gold dust. When that fell into the water and scattered over the sea bed, it was really gone and lost for ever.

"Don't be so downcast," he added gently, looking into John's gloomy face. "You're developing gold fever, and that can be a dangerous bug.

"Always remember that the Cariboo gold didn't last very long, but the people it brought here made this province. British Columbia was mostly wilderness till 1858, when gold was found and people rushed here from all over the world. It was the gold that drew them, sure. But when the gold was gone, the people stayed on and settled the land. That's

why the Cariboo story is important, John —
for the people, not for the gold."

He stopped, but John didn't answer. He had
heard every word the captain spoke, but the
words had about as much meaning as if they'd
been spoken in a foreign language. Maybe if
John had never seen the box with James
Gregor's initials on it, if he hadn't been so sure
it contained the lost gold . . .

Probably he should have known that Cariboo gold had been kept in leather pouches, not
in tin boxes. But he had wanted so badly to
believe. He had been so full of the dream of
announcing to his parents: "I've found the
gold. All your money worries are over." In his
imagination he had lived the scene so many
times — and now it would never happen.

"You have no reason to be disappointed,
John." The captain was speaking again. "You
should be very happy at what you have
achieved tonight. You've solved the mystery
and broken the conspiracy against the island.
When Greaves and Abbott read in the newspaper about the diary, they'll realize there's
no gold here and they won't come any more.
In fact, they'll probably be worried about getting into trouble, and I won't be surprised if
they disappear for a while.

"But other people will start appearing, John.

With all the publicity about the diary, there'll be lots of people wanting to see the island, and when they find out how beautiful it is, the rumors will soon be forgotten. You'll have all the vacationers you can handle — and that's what you hoped for, isn't it? Wasn't that your idea, to make the island into a vacation resort? You weren't thinking of gold when you first wanted to live here, were you?"

John shook his head. He knew that Captain Sam was right. He knew his words were sensible. But knowing and feeling were two different things, and in spite of everything, John couldn't feel happy. Deep inside he could only feel disappointment.

"Things will look better tomorrow," the captain said. "In the meantime, I'm going to tape up your foot. Then to sleep with you! You're too tired to think straight right now."

Dutifully John laid his head on the pillow. But tired as he was, it was a long time before he could stop thinking and close his eyes. When he finally did fall asleep, he dreamed of golden nuggets as big as walnuts, and coarse yellow flakes skimmed from the tops of pans.

Sun was streaming through the floathouse windows when he woke late the next morning. He heard voices, and looking up, he saw Captain Sam sitting by the radio telephone.

138

"Hi there, John." The captain sounded cheerful and happy. "I've just been talking to a friend in Victoria. He's been doing a little investigating for me, and do you know what he found out?"

"What?" John asked, but he never heard the answer because just then Linda came rushing through the door.

"Ricky's missing!" She sounded scared and breathless. "I've looked everywhere but I can't find him, and when I went to the beach I saw that his raft wasn't there. You know that raft he was making from pieces of driftwood —"

"Oh, my gosh!" The captain jumped to his feet. "Trying to keep track of you kids is like looking after a three-ringed circus! What's going to happen next?"

As he strode toward the door with Linda behind him, John called after them, "Did you look in the root cellar?"

"Of course I did!" Linda sounded indignant. "That was the first place I went."

Then they were gone and John was left alone. Even though he had a bum ankle, he wasn't going to stay here doing nothing while they searched for Ricky. His foot felt much better this morning and the elastic bandage gave it support. With the help of a stick to lean on he was sure he could manage. Probably he couldn't get as far as the beach, but he had no intention of going there anyway. He was quite sure that Ricky would be in his favorite hideout — and though Linda had already looked, he wasn't convinced that she had searched properly.

Ricky was strange about that old root cellar. He still called it his own private place, and if anyone came to look for him there, he often hid and pretended he hadn't heard them call.

"Try to put yourself in his place," his mother had said when John complained about it. "Imagine being the youngest and smallest in the family, always being told that you can't do things that all the others are doing. Wouldn't you like to have a small place all your own where you could feel like the king of the castle?"

"I guess so." John had laughed, and after one tour of inspection to make sure that nothing was hidden there, he had left the root cellar to Ricky.

Now he approached it very quietly. If Ricky didn't hear anyone coming, there was more chance of finding him before he could hide. And John wanted very much to be the one to find his young brother.

In spite of all Captain Sam had said, he still had a feeling of failure about last night.

He still felt foolish when he thought of his excited talk about gold, which had not been gold at all. Maybe if he could find Ricky on his own while the others were searching the beach he wouldn't feel so stupid after all.

But he heard no sound as he came closer to the root cellar. The door was wide open, probably the way Linda had left it. The door was never completely closed because it had swollen from the damp, and Mr. Stafford was afraid that once it shut fast it would be hard to open again. Ricky usually kept it slightly ajar, just enough to let in light and air and still give him a feeling of privacy. But he never left it wide open when he was playing in there.

John's optimism was fading rapidly. Everything was quiet and still, with no sight or sound of a little boy. He had a sinking feeling that his hunch had been wrong, and that once more he'd failed.

But even though common sense told him that Ricky couldn't be here, he refused to give in without a thorough search. He examined all possible hiding places, behind every barrel and in each dark corner.

He had to be very careful where he stepped because the ground was pitted with holes where Ricky had been digging. The holes were small ones, since Ricky's shovel hadn't had much digging power. But they made it hard going for John with his sprained foot, especially since he was wearing his father's shoe because his own wouldn't fit over the bandage.

After he had stumbled for about the tenth time and still had found no sign of Ricky, he knew that he couldn't keep on. He would have to admit defeat. But now he was getting really worried. If Linda had looked all over the island without finding Ricky, where could he be? Was he in some kind of trouble?

John was on his way out of the root cellar, intending to struggle to the beach and help the others in the search, when his foot caught once more in one of the holes. This time he couldn't regain his balance. As he fell, his back hit the door, slamming it shut with a bang. When he tried to open it, he found that it was wedged fast and wouldn't budge.

He was trapped! He would never be able to open the door with his bare hands. He was stuck until someone came to get him out. In his frustration he banged at the door with his stick. When he stopped, he heard a small cry, a cry that came from somewhere inside the root cellar.

♦

New Life for the Old Mansion

"Ricky!" John grabbed his stick and hurriedly pulled himself to his feet. "Is that you?"

From somewhere — John couldn't tell where — a frightened little voice whimpered, "Open the door. I don't like the dark."

"The door won't open, Ricky. It's wedged. But I've got a flashlight." Quickly John switched it on, thankful he had thought to pick it up from the table before he left the float-house.

"It's still dark." Ricky's voice was a shaky quiver, and cautiously John moved in the direction of the sound.

"Where are you?" he asked. "Why don't you come out? You hide yourself away where no one can see you — and then get yourself all scared!"

John swung the flashlight up and down, but he still couldn't see where the voice was coming from. That crazy kid was always getting everyone worried with his disappearing acts.

"I can't get out," Ricky quavered. "I'm stuck in here behind the wall."

"Behind the wall!" John stared at the wooden boards that had been placed at each side of the root cellar to prevent the earth from collapsing. The boards were rotten and worm-eaten, but still standing upright.

"How did you get behind the wall?" John asked in amazement.

"I was digging a hole," Ricky said in a faint voice. "It was supposed to be a secret passage for a game I was playing. Then I heard Lin and I thought it'd be fun to hide from her — because she's always bossing me around."

"But how did you get behind there?"

"I crawled through the hole I made underneath the wall. But a lot of dirt and rocks fell down and filled up the hole, and now I can't get back out!" Ricky's voice shook and he sounded close to tears.

"Oh, Ricky, why didn't you speak up before?" John growled. "You must have heard me looking for you. If you'd said something before I fell and got the door jammed, I could have gone for some tools, or called Captain Sam."

Ricky hesitated before answering. "I wanted to get back by myself. I didn't want to tell anyone because I knew you'd all be mad at me."

In spite of his anxiety, John couldn't help smiling. How many times had he felt the same way himself, when he'd done something foolish. He'd always tried to work it out on his own if he could, rather than ask for help and get a lecture.

"Try not to be scared," he said. "I'm right here on the other side of the wall and I'll get you out somehow."

He beamed his flashlight once more around the cellar and a metal object half buried in the rubble caught the light. John swooped down to pick it up. "I've found your shovel, Ricky. I'll start digging now and make a new passage. Everything will be all right."

John started to work. But it was a slow job trying to dig with the toy shovel, which was only meant for building sand castles at the beach. He tried to hurry, knowing how Ricky must be feeling, but he didn't dare press too hard for fear of breaking the frail little spade.

He dug and scraped, dug and scraped until

he was sweating with exertion. He tossed the spade aside in disgust and tried using his bare hands. Finally he broke a piece of wood from his walking stick and tried scraping the earth with that.

Once he banged into the wall as he worked, and the shaky old boards scraped against the roof, sending a heap of earth down into the hole he had dug so laboriously.

"For Pete's sake," John muttered, hurling a clump of the fallen dirt to the other side of the cellar. "I must be trying in the wrong place. Ricky could never have dug a passage here."

Just as he was deciding to start again somewhere else, he hit a pocket of softer earth that gave way more easily. With new energy he began to scrape and dig again. "I think I'm getting somewhere now," he called out to Ricky. "There should soon be a hole big enough for you to squeeze through —"

John broke off abruptly. Clearing away the last layer of earth, he saw a large piece of wood. His arms were aching with exhaustion and his hands were beginning to blister, but he went to work again, until he had uncovered a piece of wood about three feet square and five inches thick.

His breath was coming in quick gasps now. How much farther did it go down? Was it just a piece of old lumber, or could it be something else? — something like an old box?

"Oh no, I'm not going to think about *that*!" John told himself fiercely. After last night's disappointment, he wasn't going to let his dreams run riot again. He wasn't going to imagine an old treasure chest buried under the root cellar floor. Of course, it wouldn't hurt to dig around the wood a little farther and see. . . .

"John, are you still there?"

Ricky's faltering voice brought him back to the important job at hand. "Just another minute, Rick," he called out.

John figured he had dug about a foot below the wall. He couldn't get any farther down because the wood was firmly embedded in the ground. There was no chance of prying it out without a proper tool, but there might be enough room for Ricky to crawl through if the passage were cleared a bit more on his side.

"Rick," he called, "you're going to have to do some digging now, because I can't go down any farther. I'm going to pass you the spade, and I want you to clear away that stuff that fell down. It looks pretty loose from what I can see, so it shouldn't be too hard. When you're ready let me know, and I'll try to help you through."

He could hear heavy breathing as his little brother set to work. John was breathing quite fast himself, eyeing the wood in the ground and wondering.

At the same time he was listening for Captain Sam and Linda. What were they doing so long? If only they would come back soon and give him some help. He needed a knife to cut part of the wall at the bottom and give Ricky more room. He needed a spade that would dig properly.

"Ready," Ricky called, and John braced himself.

"You're sure you want to try it, Rick? You don't want to wait till Captain Sam comes?"

"No." Ricky's voice was full of fear. "I don't want to stay here any more. I want to come out."

"All right then. Lie down on your back, and I'll lie on my stomach and grab your feet."

John's hands were like ice as they closed around Ricky's ankles. Suppose his young brother got hurt? Suppose he stuck in the middle? "Captain Sam," he hollered, but there was no answer. No help was going to come. He would have to do the job himself.

Slowly, carefully, he began to pull Ricky through the narrow passage. He talked to him softly, trying to keep him from feeling scared, easing him gently under the wall, and listening all the time for some sound overhead. Last night he had been afraid of footsteps. This morning he was praying for them.

"Nearly through," he said cheerfully. "Nearly through."

And then suddenly Rick shouted, "Stop!"

"I'm stuck," he gasped, and he wiggled and squirmed, his heels waving wildly in the air.

"Give yourself a big push," John said, "and I'll keep pulling from this side."

As he began to pull Ricky's legs again, he suddenly heard an enormous crack.

"Ricky! Are you okay?"

Just then a shower of earth flew out and Ricky's shoulders and head emerged from the passage. He sat up slowly and stared at John with a dazed look.

"Are you okay?" John asked again, brushing the dirt off his brother's face. "What was that horrible cracking sound?"

Ricky managed a grin. "It wasn't me. When I gave that big push, my elbow hit some wood. I don't know what it was."

John flashed the light down at the floor. For a moment he could only gape. There, just at the edge of the plank wall, was another board buried in the earth. It had apparently cracked beneath Ricky's impact. Through the splintered wood John could see layers of yellowed old paper.

As he stood there staring, he almost missed the very sound he had been waiting to hear — footsteps outside. He rose quickly and hopped across to the jammed door, pounding on it with both fists and yelling at the top of his voice: "Captain Sam! Linda! Captain Sam!"

The footsteps stopped, changed course.

"I'm here in the root cellar," John shouted, "and Ricky is here too. But the door's stuck and we can't get out."

After that, everything seemed to happen very quickly. Linda raced to the floathouse to get some tools, and Captain Sam pried the door open with a crowbar. He burst inside breathlessly, his blue eyes widening at the sight of Ricky all covered with dirt and standing on a broken piece of wood that was embedded in the root cellar floor.

"Well, I'll be tarred and feathered," he gasped, hoisting Ricky onto solid ground and helping him brush himself off.

Once Captain Sam was sure Ricky was all right, he didn't waste time asking for explanations. He just picked up a spade and started to dig. John grabbed another spade and began scraping away the dirt at the other side of the thick wooden slab.

Finally, with much heaving by all of them together, they pulled a heavy chest out of the ground. They glanced at each other in surprise when they saw another thick piece of wood behind it, then grabbed spades and once more started digging. When they lifted out a second chest a few minutes later, still another piece of wood was revealed.

Altogether they dug up four heavily constructed chests which had been buried beneath the root cellar floor. Then, breathing hard, they rested for a few minutes, simply staring at the big boxes. One by one they carried them outside into the sunlight. No one spoke.

Finally John took an axe and broke open each chest. He drew out layer after layer of old yellowed newspapers, then several paintings. One was of the log mansion, the way it must have looked when it was first built. Another was the view from the high crag where John had built his lookout.

There were portraits of beautiful ladies and gallant-looking gentlemen, there were miniature totem poles of argillite and abalone shell, there were tapestries beautifully woven in glowing colors, and there were ornaments of the finest glass and hand-painted china. One or two things were yellowed or mildewed, and a couple of the ornaments were broken, but the chests were so rugged and so well packed that most of their contents were in perfect condition.

Captain Sam touched each piece reverently. "Well, John," he said, "you've done it this time. You've found the lost art treasures that Lee Jang hid from the looters. When you sell these things, you'll have realized your dream of becoming rich. They're worth much more than the gold you had hoped to discover. You've really hit the jackpot this time."

The captain's face smiled, but his voice sounded funny, almost sad. John had never heard him speak that way. Captain Sam was usually enthusiastic about everything — like the diary last night and the old log mansion the first time they had met.

John could remember the captain's words: "The great hall was all aglow with fine paintings and tapestries and beautiful ornaments." He remembered the day he and Linda had stood in the big room and imagined the way it must have been long ago. He thought of his father standing in the old ballroom with dreams of the future in his eyes.

152

Then he heard his own voice saying slowly, "I don't think I want to sell these things, even if they are worth a lot of money. I think I'd rather put them back in the mansion the way they used to be. I'd like them to stay here where they belong — and maybe we could keep the diary too, for our visitors to see."

A glow seemed to spread through him as he spoke. His imagination was already working, and he could see the mansion the way it would look when they had it all fixed up. "It's going to be super," he breathed.

"It really will be super." Captain Sam beamed as though he had just received the best present of his life.

"I knew it," he chortled. "I knew you'd recover from that old gold fever. And before I forget, I've got some news for you. I started to tell you this morning, then when Linda came and told us Ricky was lost I forgot all about it."

He paused and everyone waited expectantly. "I was talking to a friend in Victoria," he went on. "I asked him to do some investigating for me, and do you know what he found out? Harry Abbott's real estate office is closed, with a "For Sale" sign on the window, and Leonard Greaves has left his boat rental job at the motel. The two rogues have both gone.

153

You must have scared them away, John, when you discovered them last night."

John's eyes lit up. This was the final touch to make his happiness complete. "Now I can tell Mom and Dad the whole story," he said.

"Let's tell them right now!" Linda was almost bursting with excitement. "Come on, John, you can call on the radio-phone. You made all the discoveries, so you can tell the news."

John felt as though he had grown a good deal taller. *John Stafford, the great discoverer.* But he knew he had not done it all by himself.

"We can all say our piece," he announced. "After all, you and Captain Sam rescued me twice. And if Ricky hadn't hidden behind the wall, I would never have found the buried chests. But" — and his voice became firm — "there's one thing I do want. The name of this island should be officially changed. I want it to be called Treasure Island from now on."